A VERY SCARY CHRISTMAS

John Ward

Scareville
Series by: John Ward

Published by Crystal Lake Publishing
Where Stories Come Alive!

www.crystallakepub.com

First publication by John Ward 2023
Current version copyright 2025 John Ward
Join the Crystal Lake community today
on our newsletter and Patreon!
https://linktr.ee/CrystalLakePublishing

Download our latest catalog here:
https://geni.us/CLPCatalog

ISBN: 978-1-964398-91-4

Cover art:
Jorge Iracheta

Follow us on Amazon:

WELCOME
TO ANOTHER

CRYSTAL LAKE PUBLISHING
CREATION

Join today at www.crystallakepub.com & www.patreon.com/CLP

I WANT
YOU
FOR
SCAREVILLE
EST
20
25
ARMY
JOIN NOW!

Prologue

What you are about to experience will send shivers down your spine. A book series that will leave you questioning everything you thought you knew about things that go bump in the night.

Are you brave enough to come along on a journey that is sure to induce fear, nightmares, and leave you questioning if it's worth leaving your bed for that midnight snack? Very well! Please be sure to buckle up and always keep your arms and legs inside the ride as we delve into....

A Very Scary Christmas

1.

Christmas is the most magical time of the year. In the Carrow household, it has always been everyone's favorite holiday. We go all out with our decorations every year, beginning the day after Thanksgiving. Whether it be our elaborate lights we hang up outside, our yard ornaments, or the giant wreath that Dad hangs up on the front of our house, it's always a spectacle.

Inside is no different. We have all sorts of displays, knick-knacks, and a couple of different Christmas trees we put up every single year.

There was a lot of excitement heading into this holiday season. I had just turned 13 over the summer, so to me, it meant this was going to be the best and luckiest Christmas of all. Everything was panning out perfectly.

All was right in the world. It was Friday, and winter break had officially begun in Jamestown, New York. We lucked out this year because Christmas Day fell on the next Friday. So, it felt like a longer winter break than usual.

It's been a tradition, over the past few years, for Mom to pick my brother and me up from school on the last day before winter break. She usually takes us to the mall to get into the Christmas spirit. Today was no different.

Mom drove an SUV with third row seating. She kept it folded-down on days like today so there'd be more room for toting around newly bought Christmas decorations.

"Ooh! Mom, do you think we can go to Swerve?" my little brother Colby howled in excitement, his expression hopeful.

Swerve was a video game store at the mall. Colby knew how much I loathed video games, and I knew the only reason he asked was to annoy me.

"Sure, we can! Just remember we can't stay too long. Your father is getting in tonight, and I want to grab dinner before he gets home," she replied.

I rolled my eyes while Colby stuck his tongue out at me. Colby acted like a real jerk sometimes. He's 11 years old, but there are times I swear he acts like a total eight-year-old.

"You're a brat!" I spat in annoyance, igniting a verbal war between Colby and me.

"Kids! Enough!" Mom growled. "This is not the holiday spirit. Kelsey, be nice to your brother."

"But Mom!" I pleaded frantically as Colby smirked and stuck his tongue out at me once again.

"No buts. Now we are going to get along, and we are going to get into the Christmas spirit!" she demanded, turning the volume dial up on the radio to drown out any potential arguments.

Jingle Bell Rock began blaring through the speakers as we zoomed through town and towards Jamestown Mall. I shot an annoyed glance over at my little brother. His face was filled with glee as he happily danced to the music. I sighed in defeat and turned to look out my window.

The sun was buried behind thick grey clouds. A light dusting of snow covered most everything on this chilly winter afternoon. I couldn't help but be inspired by the spirit everyone in our community shows this time of year.

There was always such a huge variety of decorations—from inflatables to incredible lighting displays—some that even synced up to music! I wasn't sure if every other city went all out on decorating for the holidays like our town, but Jamestown was truly a sight to behold this time of year.

Finally, we arrived at the mall. Traffic was backed up. Everyone was frantically trying to turn into the parking lot and were meandering through the rows and rows of cars, just trying to luck out and find an available spot. Mom turned the radio down, as if that was going to help her to focus.

After what felt like an eternal loop of going up and down rows of cars, I could sense Mom's frustration building. She began muttering curse words under her breath.

"Christmas spirit, Mom!" I cried sarcastically. Even Colby got a chuckle out of my joke.

I saw her glare in the rearview mirror. It shot directly into my soul. I could tell she wanted to fire back a response but choked it down as she began aggressively humming a Christmas carol while continuing to search for a place for us to park.

On the far outskirts of the property, she finally managed to find a spot to pull into. Colby and I excitedly exited while Mom sat in the car for a moment and let out a sigh of relief.

The wind whipped through the vast parking lot as snow flurries began to flutter from the sky, blowing across the pavement like spilled grains of salt on the dining room table.

It was the type of cold that cut through all your layers of clothing. We trotted as a family toward the mall as fast as our legs could muster, watching out for traffic along the way.

"Brrrr! Sheesh, it's cold out there!" Mom stammered as we made our way through the doors and into the mall.

Colby and I couldn't help but agree as we brushed the light snowflakes off ourselves and made our way into the warm halls inside.

Frosty the Snowman blared through the speakers lining the hallways as families excitedly scurried from store to store. Everyone had wide eyes and smiles on their faces. The windows outside the stores were all decorated with fancy Christmas lights and different holiday-themed signage, beckoning people to come inside and see what they had to offer.

Sometimes I think Mom started this tradition to get some last-minute gift ideas for my brother and me, but it was still a great tradition, nonetheless. I don't think we were the only ones, as the mall was packed with families from all over the area.

"Mom! Mom! Let's go to Swerve!" Colby exclaimed as he eagerly sprinted a short distance ahead of Mom and me.

"Colby! Slow down and watch out for other people!" Mom barked before looking down at me. "Look honey, I know you don't like Swerve, but we'll be sure to go into any store you want after, deal?"

"Deal," I said begrudgingly as we made our way to the crowded video game store.

I took a seat on one of the benches inside the store while Colby darted around like a Tasmanian devil.

I glanced out at all the happy families making their way around the mall. There was just something about the Christmas season that made me happy. I wasn't sure if it was the music, the decorations, the quality time with family, or any of the other multitude of fun things that happened this time of year. It seemed to bring a lot of people together. I knew not everyone got the same level of enjoyment this time of year, but I wished everyone could feel the indescribable feeling that resided in the pit of my stomach this close to the holiday.

"Kelsey?" I heard my mom say, snapping me out of the trance-like state I'd been in. "Ready to go?"

"Y-Yeah! Sorry, I zoned out for a second," I replied, not realizing how long I must have been out of it.

"That's okay, honey," she replied warmly as she patted my shoulder, escorting my brother and me out of Swerve. "What store would you like to go to?"

I paused for a second, mulling over the decision. "Ooh! We could go into Rogue Outfitters!" I beamed, much to Colby's chagrin.

Rogue Outfitters was the new hit clothing company for girls that had just opened last year. Anyone who was anyone in school rocked Rogue Outfitters. From the cutest tops, jeans, hoodies, sweats, and shoes. You could find your perfect style there.

"Ew...why?" Colby said.

"Colby, your sister waited patiently when you wanted to go to Swerve. You can at least return the favor," Mom stated with a stern tone. Both Colby and I knew better than to press our luck with it.

"Fine," Colby grunted, holding his head low.

As we marched past a line of families waiting to get their picture taken with Santa, I couldn't help but crack a smile at Colby not getting his way—for once.

Santa was sitting on a giant throne, surrounded by a couple of elves, and seemed as jolly as could be, belting out his "Ho Ho Ho's" and letting out belly laughs as he asked kids what they wanted for Christmas.

I overheard the small boy on Santa's lap say he wanted a lightsaber for Christmas. I couldn't help but chuckle as we strolled past. Magical time of year indeed.

After cutting our trip to Rogue Outfitters short, thanks to Colby acting like a holy terror, we stopped in a couple other stores that Mom wanted to look at. Then, we made our way out of the mall.

As we were getting ready to exit, she glanced down at Colby and me and said, "Alright, one more trip to make, guys!"

Colby and I knew exactly what she meant. We were heading to the flea market. It was another tradition our parents started when we were younger. They wanted us to pick out a new Christmas decoration to bring home and add to the collection.

The flea market was great. There were always unique hand-made decorations you couldn't find at any store in town.

Colby and I argued about who was going to find the cooler decoration, which caused Mom to chuckle and shake her head. And with that, we made our way out as the snow began to fall a little harder.

I couldn't help but marvel at the landscape as we made our way to the flea market. Night fell quickly this time of year, and now all the houses in town were lit up with bright and vibrant displays.

I really enjoyed Christmas lights and always found myself mesmerized by how cool they looked, especially when the snow was falling.

When we finally reached the flea market, I felt a twinge of excitement in the pit of my stomach. This was one of my favorite things to do for Christmas.

The snow was really starting to come down as we hurried toward the old warehouse that had been converted into this store. Outside the entrance was an old red wagon with yellow Christmas lights strung around it, and a fully decorated Christmas tree sitting atop the wagon. Carols played through a speaker below it, and the lights, synced with the music, danced. Snow clung to its branches in a whimsical way that looked straight out of a storybook.

Once inside the store, I felt the warmth in my heart as excitement fluttered. I looked over at Colby, who seemed to be sharing the same nostalgic feeling as his eyes surveyed the area. Our mom looked down at us with a prideful smile as we ventured into the store.

There were different booths set up with some of the most beautiful handmade decorations you could ever find. From carefully constructed Christmas wreaths to fancy ornaments, there was something for everyone.

There was something special about seeing everyone's creativity on display for our community to rummage through and buy.

"Oh wow!" Mom gasped, throwing a hand over her mouth with wide eyes as she noticed a well-lit booth nearby. It had a sign hanging above it, multi-colored lights strobing. The sign read, *The Magic of Christmas by Madame Trudeau.*

The three of us quickly scampered over to her booth, while a group of older ladies slowly made their way out.

"This is so cool!" I exclaimed in bewilderment as we made our way inside.

Colby quickly bolted toward the back corner of the large booth, while Mom and I took our time taking everything the store had to offer in.

It was truly a spectacle. There were so many unique decorations throughout the room. Several fully decorated Christmas trees lined the store wall directly to the right, each one with a different theme. They were covered in different glass bulb ornaments that had to be seen to be believed. The other side wall was covered in different wreaths, some with hand-crafted little birds residing inside, and other wreaths with little berries clinging to the branches.

There was a tree in the center of the room as well, larger than the rest. It was, again, decorated to the brim with amazing ornaments-strands of garland in a variety of Christmas-themed colors wrapped around the tree.

Below the tree, a model train raced around its base, the whistle blaring as it did so. There were also a host of different handmade Nutcracker dolls hovering around the tree trunk inside the train track. Nutcrackers had always been my favorite Christmas decoration for as long as I could remember.

My eyes grew wide as I gripped my mom by her elbow and pointed. "Mom! Look!" I exclaimed as we raced over to the large tree.

As soon as we made our way over, I immediately fell in love with the assortment of Nutcracker dolls standing before me.

Before I could get a word in, an older woman slowly came around from the other side of the tree.

"Well, hello there!" she said in an excited, albeit shaky, voice. It reminded me of how my grandma would greet us when she came to visit.

The woman was dressed in an old red sweater, black slacks, and a black shawl that wrapped around her upper body just like the garland on the Christmas tree. She also had an old, colorful floral headscarf that was wrapped under her chin. It rested on top of her head--*probably to keep her hair dry from the snow*, I thought.

"Oh! Hi!" my mom replied clutching at her chest, clearly startled by this woman's sudden appearance.

"I'm Madame Trudeau, it's nice to meet you," she said in a slow, drawn-out tone, still smiling as she extended a friendly hand to my mom.

"Sarah...Sarah Carrow. Nice to meet you as well!" my mom replied as she accepted the handshake.

"Are you looking for anything in particu..." her voice trailed off. She had been interrupted by my brother noisily frolicking in excitement as he rushed back over to us. He carried something in his hands.

"Oh, well hello there," Madame Trudeau said with a surprised chuckle.

Colby shot her an indifferent side-eyed glance as he hurried over to Mom to show her what he had picked out.

"Look, Mom!" Colby cried as he held out the box to her.

"The three Jolly Elves, eh?" she said, studying the box inquisitively.

"Oh-ho-ho! Yes, those little guys are some of my favorites!" Madame Trudeau interjected.

Mom continued to survey the box, likely trying to find a price. She must have found it, because her eyes about bulged out of her head. Just as she started to say something, her cell phone began ringing.

She handed the box back to Colby and glanced at her phone.

"Shoot! It's Debbie! I forgot about the sleepover tomorrow," she cried out, fumbling to answer the phone, but not before saying, "Honey, that's fine. I'll be right back. I gotta take this call. Kelsey, feel free to pick something out. I will be right back."

And with that, Mom rushed out of the booth to take the call. Debbie was my best friend Amanda's mom.

A couple of weeks back, our parents had arranged for us to have a sleepover. I got to have my best friend over, and Colby got to have his annoying best friend, Matt over.

I couldn't help but scowl at my little brother. He was dancing around the booth like he was in the midst of a sugar rush, undoubtedly trying to rub his find in my face.

"Look what I found, Kels!" Colby beamed. "Check it out! Alfie, Charlie, and Ernie. Those are their names according to the box."

I rolled my eyes as Colby pridefully shoved the box into my stomach. I glanced down and sure enough, there were three elves in the packaging. One was wearing a red elf suit and hat--he had red hair poking out from under his hat, big blue eyes, and an eerily happy smile. His name was Alfie. The other two elves looked somewhat similar. Charlie was dressed in an all-green elf suit. He had blonde hair, hazel green eyes, and a rather evil-looking smirk on his face. The final elf, Ernie, was clad in all white with a silver belt. He had white hair, brown eyes, and a white, wispy beard dangling from his chin.

"Y-yeah. They do seem to be jolly," I lied.

Sure, they were elves, but their menacing grins and their weird, big eyes staring blankly at me gave me the chills. I quickly handed Colby his box back and he went back to celebrating once more.

Madame Trudeau stood awkwardly between us, seemingly unsure of how to approach Colby's erratic behavior.

"Do you need help picking anything out?" she inquired.

"Oh...I uh – No, I should be able to find something. Thank you though." I replied softly, shooting an evil glare at Colby.

"Very well." Madame Trudeau stated calmly before turning toward Colby. "I will just hold onto this for now until you all are ready to check out."

I let out a happy chuckle at the dismay on my brother's face as Madame Trudeau yanked the package away from him and walked out of sight to the back of the booth.

"That was great!" I taunted, poking the disappointed Colby in his chest.

"Whatever." He fired back before storming away and out of sight.

I couldn't help but gloat in that situation. Colby always got what he wanted. I guess that was a perk of being the youngest.

Now it was my time to search for something neat to bring home. I began to circle my way around the giant Christmas tree, following the same path as the whistling train as it rode by. My eyes lit up when I noticed a package with a trio of Nutcracker dolls. They stood about a foot tall, similar to the elves.

All the nutcrackers had black fuzzy caps atop their heads, but had different colored outfits on. The first one had a blue top with red fringe and gold buttons, along with a pair of white pants and black boots. The next had on a red top, white fringe accents, and black buttons, with blue pants and black boots. The final one had a green top, gold fringe, gold buttons, and a pair of red pants to go with his red boots. They were perfect!

Just as I was about to grab the box, I heard a strange noise come from the rear of the store. Figuring it must be Colby trying to play a prank—like always—I crept my way around the tree to try to flip the prank on him, but he wasn't there.

With confusion setting in, I was about to leave until I heard it again. It sounded like an aggressive whisper. *What was it?*

I glanced around and noticed Madame Trudeau standing behind her desk. Her eyes were closed, and I could see her lips moving to the whispering sounds I'd heard earlier. She waved her hands around in the air.

When her eyes opened and stared directly at me, I felt a jolt of paralyzing fear surge through me, like hopping into ice water. My heart immediately began racing. I slowly backed away from her and her desk, unsure of what I had just witnessed.

My stomach erupted with an explosion of nerves. They shot through my whole body like a cannon blast when she flashed a creepy smile, her eyes still cold and dark.

I nearly jumped out of my shoes when I heard, "Kelsey?" come from behind me. I turned around in fright and noticed my mom standing next to the tree, a confused expression on her face.

I quickly turned my gaze back to Madame Trudeau, who was now busily sorting through a box of Christmas trinkets.

"Is everything okay?" Mom asked, her voice concerned.

"Huh? Y-yeah. Everything's okay Mom," I replied.

"Well okay silly, did you find anything you wanted?" she questioned with a hearty chuckle.

"Yeah, I actually did..." I said, trying to shake off what I just seen.

What had I just witnessed? I must have zoned out, because Mom called out my name again, snapping me out of it.

"Well, are you going to show me?" she asked incredulously, shaking her head with another laugh as I led the way over to the Nutcrackers I had found.

Mom bent down to look at the packaging. I saw her look at the price tag on the box and then glance down with a woeful look.

"I'm sorry, honey. I know how much you love Nutcracker dolls. I just don't think I can swing both trio sets right now," she said in a sorrowful tone as she set the box back down. "Is there anything else you'd like?"

I couldn't believe it. Colby was getting what he wanted *again*, while I was left feeling dejected.

I let out an exasperated sigh. "Let me look," I replied sadly.

I really wanted those Nutcracker dolls. How was I supposed to top Colby's decoration now? I glanced around the room, and nothing really caught my eye. I could feel myself fighting back tears. I knew Christmas wasn't about decorations or gifts, but we always have so much fun with it, so being told "no" hurt. Not to mention, I didn't like losing to Colby.

Finally, giving in to defeat, I meandered over to a snow globe resting on a shelf. Inside, it had a warm-looking cottage nestled in the middle of a snow-covered forest. I gave it a shake and watched the beautiful snowflakes flutter around the glass ball.

It wasn't *as cool* as Colby's choice, but I had always liked snow globes. They were so peaceful to stare into.

I quietly walked over to Mom and handed her the snow globe. Colby came out from behind her, a grin on his face.

"*That's* what you chose? That's so dumb! Looks like I win!" Colby sniggered and cheered.

"Shut up!" I yelled and started to storm toward him before Mom got between us, throwing up a cautionary hand to stop me.

"Colby, this time of year isn't about winning," she scolded with that same stern tone we both knew not to tempt fate with. "Apologize to your sister. That was very rude. One more comment like that and you aren't getting your elves."

Colby pouted, staring at the floor while dragging his foot to and fro. He gave me a weak apology and walked away in the opposite direction.

"Honey, your snow globe is beautiful. They were always my favorite growing up. I think it is a wonderful piece to add to our tradition," Mom said with motherly approval.

"Thanks, Mom," I replied, still fighting back tears, but feeling a little better.

We walked back up to the register where we were met with a warm smile from Madame Trudeau. Her smile and her face appeared different now than it had when I saw whatever she was doing earlier.

My stomach was in knots as we stood at the register. When I saw Madame Trudeau glance over at me, I had to quickly look away. Maybe it was nothing, but something about her felt off.

I was so excited when Mom had finished paying and we were finally able to leave the store.

"Take good care of those elves!" Madame Trudeau called out as we made our way toward the exit.

Mom and Colby both let out a chuckle and simultaneously said "We will."

I, however, felt a chill creep down my spine at Madame Trudeau's words.

"One more pit stop to make before home guys, I'm sorry," Mom said as she pulled into the local grocery store a few minutes from our house. "I just need to grab a couple things for dinner really quick."

"Okay, Mom," we both replied as she got out of the SUV and locked the car doors. She disappeared into the snowy abyss and headed for the entrance.

"Alright, let's see here," Colby said as he unbuckled his seatbelt and began to rummage through the bags in the backseat, pulling out his box of Jolly Elves.

"I don't think Mom would like you opening that right now," I spat in annoyance.

"What? Why would she care?" he asked, sounding offended by the thought.

"Sure, what do I know?" I scoffed and turned to look out my window.

"Look! It even says they're from the North Pole!" Colby exclaimed, completely ignoring my warning as he pointed at the front of the packaging.

I rolled my eyes and responded sarcastically, "Oh, that's so cool, Colby."

What a dumb gimmick. As if these elf dolls were *actually* from the North Pole.

"Whatever, you're just jealous," he replied as he tore the box open and began peeling the elf dolls out of their plastic slots from behind me.

"*My name is Kelsey, and I'm a giant doofus,*" I could hear Colby say in a squeaky, albeit raspy, voice, trying to imitate what he thought an elf might sound like.

I turned to look at Colby. He held the elf with the red suit, the one known as Alfie, just inches from my face. I looked into Alfie's big, haunting eyes and creepy smile as Colby began making him dance around in the air.

"*I love Christmas, how 'bout you?*" Colby said in the same voice. He continued to make the elf dance right by my face.

"Knock it off, Colby," I interjected, beginning to get annoyed.

"*Oh...is someone mad they got a stupid snow globe?*" he joked once again in the same ridiculous elf voice.

"I said *enough*, Colby," I roared, angrily swatting his hand, sending Alfie flying from his grip and into the back of the SUV.

"Sheesh! What'd ya do that for?" he cried out as he leapt up to look back and make sure Alfie was okay.

"You were being a jerk. Besides, those things are creepy anyhow," I said coldly, turning toward my window once again. I wished Mom would hurry up.

"*We are not creepy*!" Colby said in his gritty elf voice again.

I glanced over my shoulder and saw him holding up the elf in white, Ernie, this time. Elves were meant to be happy, but something about these dolls' faces and Colby using the creepiest voice imaginable, were enough. I did not want any part of these little elves.

"Get it away from me, Colby. I mean it!" I demanded, rearing my hand back in a threatening manner again.

"*Sheesh. Party pooper*," he replied with his elf voice, this time in a lower register as he placed Ernie back in his slot.

Colby then got up and twisted around to look in the back of the car. "Hey, where's Alfie?"

"Stop it, Colby," I yelled.

"No. Kels, I'm serious. I can't find him anywhere," he replied urgently as he began fumbling around with the different bags.

I let out a deep exhale as I unbuckled my seatbelt. "Colby, if this is another one of your pranks, so help me God."

I hopped up on the backseat as we both began to dig around the back of the car. Colby was right, Alfie was nowhere to be found. Granted, it would have been easier with some sort of light.

"Oh! Here he is!" Colby declared as he hunched over the back of his seat by the corner of the folded down third-row seats.

Something didn't add up. When I'd swatted Alfie out of Colby's hand, he had flown into the far back of the car. He was now somehow up by Colby's seat. I could feel my heart frantically flutter as I tried to choke out the words.

"H-how did he wind up over there?" I asked, my breathing becoming more rapid.

"I don't know, he probably bounced around and landed there. Stop being weird," Colby said dismissively as he checked to make sure Alfie hadn't been damaged.

I couldn't wrap my mind around it. The thought of it defied the laws of physics. I couldn't think of a way Alfie could have flown to the far back and then bounced back toward our seats.

"*Yeah Kelsey, stop being weird,*" I heard Colby belt out in his disturbing elf voice once more before stuffing Alfie in his place in the plastic holder and sliding the elves back into the box.

"You're such a brat," I stated in disgust as Mom flung the driver's door open.

"Alright, guys. All set. Let's go get dinner made and see your father," she declared as she fired up the car. Once again, she had us on the road, barreling through the snowstorm.

After seeing what Madame Trudeau had done at the flea market, and having the strange occurrence in the car, I didn't know if I was going crazy or not. I couldn't put my finger on it, but there was *something* wrong with those elves. I could feel it.

"Oh, look at that, Dad's home!" Mom exclaimed as we pulled into our now snow-covered driveway.

Dad was a long-haul truck driver. He worked long hours and drove all over the country throughout most of the year *to provide for his family,* as he always said. We always missed him while he was gone but had grown to understand that he worked hard so that we could have an easier life.

He must have seen our headlights through one of the windows in the house as we pulled in, because he came sprinting out the front door in his coat, jeans, and work boots. He trudged through the deepening snow with bright eyes and an excited smile, not caring about the cold or the giant snowflakes hitting him.

Dad met us at the car as soon as Mom put it into park, eagerly waiting to greet us as we got out. He promptly gave Mom a hug, and then a quick smooch on the lips, to which Colby said "Ew, gross!"

Mom and Dad couldn't help but chuckle as they ended their embrace and Dad excitedly scooped Colby up in a big bear hug.

"Hey, champ!" Dad exclaimed as he swayed back and forth with Colby in his arms. "Have you been behaving?"

"Eh, I'm doin' my best, Dad," he replied, which elicited an eye roll from me and another chuckle from Mom.

"And there's my girl. I've missed all of you so much!" Dad said as he ran over and gave me a big hug as well.

"We missed you too, Dad," I replied, taking in his warm, comforting embrace.

"What a perfect night to get home," he said as he turned and brought us all together in a family embrace. We took in the sight of our home.

The way our house looked, all lit up, with giant flakes of snow coming down, was like something off a Christmas card. It reminded me of the snow globe I had picked out earlier.

We had begun decorating the house the day after Thanksgiving. It was another of our family traditions, and we always got into the Christmas spirit as early as possible.

We lived in a simple two-story red brick house with an attached garage that neither of our parents could park in because it had collected a lot of other stuff over the years. The front of our house was lined by a mulch bed with bushes that stood a couple feet off the ground. Gold lights were intertwined through each bush, and their branches had begun to accumulate snow.

We had hung multicolored string lights with giant bulbs over the entire roof of the house and garage, and had several yard inflatables dancing in the windy, snowy night.

"This is what it's all about. This is the beauty of Christmas," Dad said, with a prideful smile on his face as his eyes surveyed the area, taking everything in with us at his side.

"Uh...David, not to be a downer, but it's freezing. Do you think we could head inside?" Mom asked through clattering teeth and a big, hopeful smile.

"Oh! Uh, yes, I'm so sorry!" he apologized, letting out a hearty chuckle as we began to disband.

"Dad, wait 'til you see the decoration I picked out!" Colby exclaimed as he raced to the back of Mom's SUV. He grabbed the bag containing the Christmas decorations while Mom and I grabbed the rest of the stuff to bring inside.

"Is that right, champ?" Dad asked excitedly. He took the bags from Mom and me and carried them inside for us.

7.

"Alright, dinner is served!" Mom hollered from the kitchen.

Mom had been busily working away making Dad's favorite dinner, chicken parmesan, while the three of us sat in our living room watching the original *How the Grinch Stole Christmas*. Before starting the movie, Colby and I had both showed Dad our decoration choices for this year.

Of course, Dad showed appreciation for both as we set them up on display.

Our living room, much like the rest of our house, was covered in Christmas decorations. It was a pretty large, rectangular living room.

We had a huge bay window in the center of the far wall, our TV stand sat catty-corner to it in the corner of the room, and a fireplace sat directly left of the TV stand. Our Christmas tree stood between the TV stand and our bay window.

Our living room was the focal point where we spent a lot of time as a family this time of year. Even more trinkets were displayed all around here.

The tree was decorated with an assortment of different colored ornaments and lights that were set to change colors through a timed system. It had red, gold, and white garland draped around it, and a red and green-colored flannel tree skirt beneath it. Several gifts were already wrapped and tucked underneath it. Lastly, we had a ladder decoration leaning against the tree with a Santa Claus doll that would climb up and down, dragging a strand of Christmas lights behind him.

We had decorated the mantle above our fireplace with small ceramic houses, my snow globe, and had even added Colby's elf dolls. Stockings hung from the face of the mantle, eagerly waiting to be filled on Christmas morning.

When Mom called us in for dinner, we had to snap out of the Christmas-like trance we were in from watching the Grinch. Colby groaned, while Dad, who was obviously hungry, hopped right up and eagerly ushered us toward the dining room.

"I am going to bring the elves with me," Colby stated earnestly.

"Ugh. Do you have to?" I whined.

"Kelsey, it's fine," Dad said, obviously trying to diffuse a potential argument so we could sit down and eat.

As we entered the dining room, Mom had already portioned all our plates. We sat at our seats while Colby set up his elves on the corner of the table next to him, so they were sitting in a way where they could *see everyone.*

"Do they *have* to sit on the table?" I asked in annoyance.

"Where else would they sit?" Colby quizzed.

"Anywhere else. They're *creepy*," I sneered.

"Kelsey, Colby, that's enough!" declared Mom, clearly sick of our arguing over the Jolly Elves.

Dad, who had been hungrily chomping away at his food, glanced up and noticed the glare Mom was shooting at him. He quickly swallowed his bite, almost choking as he let out a cough.

"Kelsey, they're just elves. They're friendly and make gifts for kids on Christmas. How could they be creepy?" he said in a careless manner. He nodded to Mom and took another bite of his pasta.

I let out a sigh, giving up. I knew it wasn't worth the argument. It all had to be in my head anyhow. Sure, the thing with Madame Trudeau was creepy, but maybe she had just been meditating. Who knows?

Even still, I couldn't help but glance up and notice the elves staring at me from across the table. It felt like their eyes were glued to me. I began to eat faster, feeling a little uncomfortable.

"Oh boy, that was some delicious chicken parm," Colby said in his squeaky, yet abrasive elf voice.

"Can you knock it off with the weird elf voice already?" I wailed, slamming my fork down on my plate.

"*Oh...someone wants to be on the naughty list this year. Bad Kelsey. Bad!*" he cried in that eerie voice once more, shaking Charlie the green elf at me aggressively.

"Mom!" I shouted, shooting an angry scowl in her direction.

"Colby, go put the elves back on the mantle and rinse your plate off," she said with an exasperated exhale.

"Fine," he surrendered as he grabbed the trio of elves and walked them back into the living room.

Finishing my plate felt much easier, now that I no longer had the three goons staring at me from across the table.

After dinner, we all helped clean up the dishes, and then wrapped up the night by playing a couple of board games before heading off to bed. All in all, it was a great way to start winter break. We were all so excited that Dad was home.

As I made my way through the living room and toward the staircase to head up to my room, I looked back at the smiling elves staring at me from across the way. A shiver ran down my spine as I made my way upstairs and out of their line of sight.

8.

Once in the comfort of my room, I quickly changed into my pajamas.

I guess you could say I'm a little spoiled. My bedroom had everything a girl my age could ever ask for. I had my bed, which was in the center wall of my room, and nightstands on both sides. One held a lamp and some of my favorite books, the other had a fishbowl with my pet goldfish, Hank. I also had a desk with a computer where I could do some of my schoolwork or watch videos online.

Across from my bed, sitting above a standing dresser in the corner, was my little TV. Next to it was a small bench facing my bed between that dresser and my closet. Posters of my favorite bands and movies also lined the walls of my room.

I flipped back the covers on my bed and promptly flopped onto it like a sack of potatoes. I got myself nice and comfy, turned on the TV, and turned off my lamp.

I scrolled through the channels until I came across another one of my favorite Christmas movies, *Home Alone.* This movie always cheered me up.

After the movie ended, I could feel my eyelids growing heavy. I knew it was time for bed. I shut the TV off and drifted off to sleep.

I don't know how long I had been sleeping, but something caused me to stir awake in the middle of the night. I groggily rolled toward my bedroom door.

I could hear what sounded like Colby talking in his ominous and scratchy elf voice.

I blinked my eyes rapidly and rubbed them, trying to wake up as I sat up in my bed. It sounded like multiple voices. They all sounded similar. They all had that same squeaky, gravelly tone that Colby had used earlier in the day.

I glanced over at my computer. It was set for the monitor to sleep but display the time floating around on the screen when not in use. It was 1:17 AM. There was no way Colby could still be awake. Mom and Dad would kill him if they knew he was up.

I sat in silence for another few moments. The conversation was still going, and my agitation began to grow. I couldn't believe Colby would stoop to this level, trying to scare me in the middle of the night. He should know better.

I ripped off my bed covers and crept toward my bedroom door. I placed my ear to the wood to hear better. Sure enough,

I could hear the shuddersome voices talking back and forth, seemingly down the hall from my room.

I let out a frustrated sigh. I didn't want to wake my parents because they would be furious. But enough was enough.

I slowly opened my bedroom door and peeked out. It was pitch black in the hallway where all our bedrooms branched out. Suddenly, something changed.

Silence.

"Colby?" I whispered hoarsely.

Silence.

"Colby this isn't funny!" I croaked in a hushed voice.

The silence remained. Now, I was starting to worry. My heart raced as apprehension started to build. I had never been afraid of the dark, but this time, *something* felt different.

I took a cautious step out of my room and turned toward Colby's bedroom once more. The silence was deafening. The only sound permeating within our walls was the heat blasting through the air vents.

"Colby!" I hissed, once again to no response.

It suddenly became harder to breathe, as if a vacuum had sucked all the air out of the hallway. My breathing grew more shallow and rapid. I had heard the phrase "cutting the tension with a knife" and was never really able to comprehend what that meant until this very moment.

Both the crippling fear of waking my parents and the fear of roaming around in the darkness were daunting, to say the least. I slowly tiptoed further down the hall. Suddenly, the floorboard beneath my foot creaked loudly under my weight. It sent a jolt of fear through me as I had not expected the sudden noise.

I took a deep breath to compose myself in the dark, silent hallway. Finally, I made it to Colby's room. The door was closed. I pressed my ear to it and heard nothing.

I carefully twisted the doorknob and pushed the door open, doing my best to prevent it from making any creaking noises.

What I saw when I peered into the room completely blew me away. Colby was sleeping in his bed. *It couldn't be.*

"Colby?" I whispered.

He didn't respond or stir in his slumber. I didn't know whether he was pulling a fast one on me, or if he was legitimately sleeping.

"Hey, loser!" I said quietly. Still no response.

Caught in total confusion, I stood in his doorway for a few moments longer. It was still dead silent. Nothing was stirring, not even a mouse.

Dumbfounded, I slowly closed his bedroom door, cautious not to make any noises. As soon as the door silently shut, I turned and began to head back toward my room. I was careful to make sure I missed the creaky floorboard this go around.

My heart was still racing, and my mind was clouded. Had I been hearing things? Had Colby played a prank on me? Either way, I wasn't sure. I just knew I wanted to go back to bed and get a fresh start in the morning.

As I reached the doorway to my bedroom, I froze once again as I heard the TV in my room turn on. I couldn't begin to articulate the wave of sheer electric shock that coursed through my body. I felt all the hairs on my arm and the back of my neck stand up, goosebumps forming all over.

I wanted to scream. I wanted to cry. I could do nothing but stand in the hallway, bursting at the seams with apprehension and dread. How had my TV just turned on? There was no way this was some elaborate prank.

Thump...Thump...Thump...Thump...Thump... My heart was beating like the high school band drumline.

Finally, I mustered the courage to put one foot in front of the other, even though it felt like I had cinder blocks attached to my feet. Determined, I turned the corner and rushed into my bedroom. To my amazement, it was empty. Nothing was to be found, and nobody was in there. I wasn't sure if I should feel relieved or terrified at that moment.

I shut the door to my bedroom and quickly rushed over to my bed. I reached across to my end table and turned the TV off. The house grew silent once more.

I pulled the covers over top of me, but I didn't feel any better. On the one hand, *maybe* a power surge caused the TV to turn on, on its own. I had heard about that happening in the past. On the other hand, it had never happened in my entire life, so how likely was it? *Especially* after hearing voices.

My brain was at war with itself, and I tossed and turned for what felt like an eternity before finally fading to sleep.

The early morning sun peered through my window in what felt like mere seconds after I had finally fallen back to sleep. My eyes felt heavy as they fluttered open as the golden sunlight beamed into my room. I could feel the sun's warmth across my face and felt it melting away all my concerns from last night.

I let out a hearty yawn as I groggily rolled over and sat up on the edge of my bed, facing my computer. It was 8:13 AM. It was a little earlier than I wanted to wake up on my first day of winter break, but I wasn't going to let that ruin my day.

My optimism was short-lived, however, when I stood up and turned toward my dresser. I let out an ear-piercing shriek that probably woke up the entire neighborhood. There, sitting on the bench in my room facing my bed, were the three Jolly Elves with their menacing smiles and horrifying big eyes staring holes right through me.

I began to sob uncontrollably as I dropped to the floor in agony. I could hear my parents come flying out of bed as they rushed toward my room.

"Kelsey, what's wrong?" my dad hollered, a look of fear and primal protection mode on his face as he and Mom raced into the room.

I couldn't even say anything. All I could do was point in the direction of my bench.

My parents looked at the bench, and then each other. They slowly turned toward my doorway.

"Colby!" they both shouted immediately.

A couple moments later, a drowsy Colby came cautiously into my room. My parents yelled at him and told him he'd taken his prank too far. Colby swore up and down that he didn't do it. I didn't know what to believe. My brother had played some cruel pranks before, but nothing like this.

They told Colby to go take the dolls back downstairs and put them on the mantle where they belonged. He held his head low as he sauntered out of my room with the elves in hand.

My parents both walked over, gave me a hug, consoled me for a couple of minutes and told me that everything was going to be okay. They told me to come downstairs with them. Dad said he was going to make his world-famous omelets for breakfast, and that Mom, Colby, and I could turn on a Christmas movie while we waited.

I nodded my head, and we made our way downstairs. Dad pulled Colby aside and had his father-son coaching moment before he headed off into the kitchen to begin making breakfast.

We had agreed to watch my absolute *favorite* Christmas movie, *The Santa Clause.* It was another one of those Christmas movies that immediately cheered me up and put me in the holiday spirit.

After we finished eating breakfast, Mom and Dad said we needed to go get dressed for our virtual Christmas family photo.

Instead of taking a family photo and mailing out cards, my parents had begun waiting until about a week before Christmas to take a family photo that my dad would doctor up on the computer and send out to family in an email. Dad reminded Colby and me every year that he hated doing it this way, but it was getting too expensive to do the old way of printing and making cards due to *inflation*. Whatever that meant.

I quickly went upstairs and threw on the outfit that Mom had picked out for me a few weeks ago. It was a white turtleneck and a red and green-colored flannel dress to wear overtop of it, with a pair of white tights underneath. She had also picked out a pair of black dressy shoes for me to wear. I wasn't a fan of them but knew I wouldn't be wearing them long.

After changing out of my pajamas, I rushed over to the bathroom to meet my mom. She said she was going to curl my hair and make it *pretty*.

"You have the most beautiful blonde hair," my mom commented as she ran the hot curling iron through my locks. "I wish my hair looked like this still."

"Aw, Mom!" I replied with a smile. She sure knew how to make me feel special.

After she had finished curling my hair, we all met downstairs. Mom had on a similar style outfit to mine, except hers was more of a red and blue flannel colored dress overtop of her white turtleneck. Dad and Colby were both wearing Christmas sweaters, khaki pants, and nice brown dress shoes.

"Agh! Dad, this thing is so itchy!" Colby complained, scratching wildly at his chest and behind his back.

"Well, the sooner we get this photo done, the sooner you can take it off," Dad replied as he took his time setting up his camera on the tripod and getting the perfect angle.

We were going to stand next to the fireplace. Dad had already stoked the fireplace earlier and had a small fire burning inside it. He rushed over and shut the blinds to the bay window, dimming the room a bit and giving it more of that evening-time feel.

Once he rejoined us, we moved next to the fireplace. I was the shortest, so I was on the far end, nearest the fireplace. Even though Colby was a couple years younger, he was already an inch taller than me.

"Ope! Darn it! Hang on guys, I forgot to set the timer," Dad said, rushing back over to his camera.

"Oh, come on Dad! This sweater is killin' me!" Colby wailed as he furiously began scratching himself once again.

"Sorry! Sorry!" Dad replied as he returned and got back in his position for the picture.

Right as the camera blinked to signal it was about to snap the photo, I felt something tug on my hair from behind.

"Ow!" I yelped right as the picture was taken.

"What? What's the matter?" Dad stammered in confusion.

"Colby pulled my hair!" I whined in shock, looking at him with repulsion.

"I-I did not! I swear!" he said, tensing up as Mom and Dad both looked down at him with daggers in their eyes.

Dad grumbled as he made his way back over to the camera. "Okay, that one's deleted. Let's try this again."

Dad rushed over, having set the timer once more. We all tried our best to smile like a big happy family as the timer began to wind down yet again. The light began to flash, signaling the picture was about to be taken.

"Ow! Colby, knock it off!" I howled in pain as my hair was pulled once again.

"I'm not doing anything!" he replied defensively.

"Alright, that's enough!" Dad yelled angrily. "I guess we are going to have to separate you two. Colby, you come stand over here next to me."

And with that, Colby walked over to his new spot for the photo while I rubbed my now sore scalp. Mom gave me a squeeze on my shoulder and a comforting look as she smiled at me letting me know it was okay.

Dad rushed over to the camera for the third time and came back for our family portrait.

"Third time's a charm," he said sarcastically, taking his spot between Mom and Colby.

"Everyone say cheese!" Mom ordered as the timer wound down.

"Cheese!" we all said in unison as the picture snapped. It went off without a hitch this time.

Dad marched over to his camera to inspect the photo. After a few seconds of surveying the photo, he glanced up at us with a smile.

"It turned out great! I think we got it!"

"Oh, thank God!" Colby yelled dramatically as he quickly ripped his sweater off and tossed it onto a nearby rocking chair.

Mom and Dad couldn't help but chuckle at Colby's antics as they gathered up the camera equipment and headed over toward the office to edit the photo and design the virtual Christmas card.

"Way to be a liar and tell Mom and Dad that I was pulling your hair!" Colby stated angrily as he started to make his way toward the staircase.

"You *did* pull my hair. Don't try to play it off like you were innocent!" I called back at him as he began to march up the steps.

"No, I didn't! I was ready to take that stupid sweater off the moment I put it on! I wouldn't pull your hair and make myself wear that thing any longer than I had to!" he yelled from the top of the stairs before slamming his bedroom door moments later.

I paused for a moment, trying to take everything in as I rubbed my scalp again. It still hurt a little bit. He did have a point. Why would he pull a prank that in turn would punish himself?

I glanced back to where our family photo took place. That's when I noticed it. The spot I was standing in for the family portrait was right next to the Jolly Elves on the mantle. Not only that, it appeared that the elf closest to where I stood, Ernie the white elf, was lying on his side as if he had been knocked over.

My heart sank. *Did Ernie pull my hair?*

10.

I couldn't stand to be in the living room any longer. I followed Colby's move and quickly made my way upstairs to my room as well. I could hear Colby in his room talking. He was clearly already playing one of his video games online.

I wanted to ask Colby if Ernie had been leaning over on his side like that the whole time, but the truth was, I didn't remember looking up at the elves through all the chaos. It was possible that Colby was just playing another prank, and that the elf had been lying like that the whole time.

On the other hand, Colby seemed pretty sincere. I wasn't sure *what* to think. I just knew I hadn't felt comfortable around those dolls since we'd brought them home. Something just felt...*off*.

I entered my room, and quickly changed out of my family photo attire, and into more comfortable clothes consisting of a hoodie and a pair of sweatpants.

I knew reading would help take my mind off things, so I walked over to my computer desk, and grabbed the fantasy book I had been reading. I plopped on the bed and began to scan the pages. The story was so captivating. I could feel myself getting lost in the story every time I read it.

In the subconscious of my mind, I could occasionally hear Colby yelling at his video game. This was both normal and annoying. It made it harder for me to focus on my story.

I placed the book down on my chest in frustration as I rubbed my eyes.

"Colby, could you keep it down? I'm trying to read!" I bellowed as I banged my fist on his wall.

Colby didn't respond but did appear to quiet down afterward. Feeling a little better, I picked my book up and began my journey into the story once more.

Finally, I was able to get lost in my book. I was at an intense chapter in the story. The princess and her knight in shining armor were battling a dragon on their journey back to their castle.

As the battle scene began to grow more intense, I found myself snapping out of my dream-like state of the story. I could hear the pitter-patter of little footsteps and whispering.

I set my book down and glanced toward my open doorway. Mom and Dad only allowed us to have our bedroom doors shut while we were sleeping or changing clothes. The rest of the time, we had to keep them open.

Everything fell silent outside my room aside from hearing the faint sound of Colby's fingers jostling the buttons and thumb sticks on his video game controller. Maybe *that* was what I had heard.

I shook my head vigorously, trying to de-fog my brain, rubbed my eyes and then picked up my book to continue reading.

A few moments passed before I heard the same noises again. I quickly dropped my book this time and shot a glance over at my doorway. Once again, things were still.

I must be losing my mind.

By now, I was starting to get irritated. I picked my book up once again and began reading. Things seemed to remain quiet as I continued through the intense chapter I was on.

Without warning, my focus on the book was disrupted once more. I heard whispering. It was closer this time.

I tried to shrug it off for a moment before I heard a light-hearted chuckle at the foot of my bed. My heart skipped a beat as a wave of cold came across my entire body. It felt as though time slowed to a crawl. Chills ran down my spine.

I slowly set my book down. What I saw next was the most terrifying thing I could ever imagine. There, at the foot of my bed sitting and staring, were the Jolly Elves. Instead of their normal creepy smiles, their expressions looked angry. Their eyebrows were slanted and they glared at me with malicious hatred burning in their eyes.

I didn't even have time to process what was happening. I quickly threw my book to the side and flew out of bed, letting out a giant shriek that rattled the very walls of our home. I sprinted as fast as I could out of my room.

11.

As I bounded down the staircase, I could hear my parents bolting around the corner. They met me at the base of the stairs.

"Honey! What's wrong?" Dad questioned, his breathing seemed shallow, eyes wide with alertness.

"The...the elves...they're *alive*!" I wailed, beginning to cry out of sheer terror as I covered my face with both hands.

There was a slight pause, and a moment of apprehensive silence as Colby came rushing toward the staircase.

"Honey. They're just dolls. Just like the snowman over there," Mom said, pointing to the snowman plush sitting on our coffee table.

"No! No! You don't understand! They came into my room and sat on my bed while I was reading!" I cried out in desperation. "And their faces...they...they looked angry!"

My parents exchanged a frustrated and skeptical glance at each other as I told them to follow me and come look.

They obliged as they followed me up the steps. Colby followed in close pursuit to see what all the ruckus was about.

"See? Look!" I said pointing to the elf dolls sitting at the foot of my bed, their backs resting against the short footboard.

The three of them looked at the elves and inspected the area.

"They look normal to me," Dad replied shortly.

"Wh-what?" I asked as I came running over.

He was right. The elves' expressions had returned to their normal, bright-eyed and wide smile-covered faces.

"That...That's not possible!" I declared frantically as I crouched down for a closer look.

"Just knock it off, Kelsey," Colby sneered. "You have been jealous ever since I got the elves. You probably brought them up here to try to get me in trouble again."

I looked over at Colby, and then back to my parents. Each of them sported the same judgmental, yet equally concerned expressions on their faces.

"I...I...Look, I know what happened. And I know what I saw!" I cried out.

I could tell by the look on their faces that they didn't believe me. My mind was going a mile a minute. None of this seemed real, and *no one* trusted what I was saying. No one said anything.

"I'm not lying!" I sobbed. "I swear!"

The look of disappointment on my parents' faces was heartbreaking.

"Colby, will you take your elves back down to the mantle, please?" Mom asked.

"Sure, Mom," Colby said, bumping his shoulder against mine on his way to scoop up his elves and leave the room.

Dad exited the room as well, no longer sensing an emergency. He told Mom he was going to go finish designing the cards, and to meet him back in the office when she was ready.

Mom pulled me aside and sat with me on my bed. She looked down at me with a worried expression on her face.

"Kelsey, if this is about the Nutcracker dolls, I am sorry," she said with a voice full of sadness.

"Mom, it's not. It's fine, I promise. But there is something seriously wrong with those elves! I didn't bring them up here, I swear!" I replied anxiously.

Mom threw up a cautionary hand.

"Kelsey, that is enough. You know how much we all love you, but this is not how a teenager acts. You know we do not tolerate temper tantrums in this household," she said sternly.

I knew I was getting nowhere trying to convince her of the legitimacy of what I just experienced. I wanted to tell her about what I saw at Madame Trudeau's store in the flea market but knew she would just actively dismiss that story as well. At this point, I was starting to look like the girl who cried wolf to them.

I swallowed my pride and told her I was sorry. There was no point in me trying to push the issue any further. Mom gave me a hug and reminded me of tonight's slumber party. She said she hoped I was excited as she got up and left my room.

The truth was, I wasn't excited. I felt alone. No one believed what was happening. I could understand why they didn't, but I knew what I was seeing, hearing, and experiencing. I felt a sense of cold dread that I couldn't shake. Almost like the body chills you get when you are sick.

Hopefully, Amanda would believe me when she got here.

12.

The rest of the day seemed to go by without any incident. I helped Mom bake cookies while Dad and Colby shoveled the snow from last night off our driveway.

Mom had lit some candles that smelled like pine trees to really bring the holiday vibes into the house. We listened to Christmas music and rolled out the cookie dough.

We made a variety of different chocolate chip cookies. Some with large chocolate chunks, and some that we mixed in peanut butter chips. We had also decided to make some no-bakes, along with sugar cookies that we put frosting and sprinkles on. Those were my favorites to make because you could be creative with them.

As the first batch of cookies came out of the oven, Dad and Colby both came inside, kicking the snow off their boots as they began to strip off their coats and gloves.

"Perfect timing," Mom said with a smile as she handed each of them a cookie wrapped in a napkin. "Careful, they're still hot."

They each appreciatively grabbed their cookies, thanking Mom and me for baking. Then, they disappeared into the living room.

As the hours continued to pass and we drew nearer to when Matt and Amanda would be arriving, Mom and I finally finished our baking for the day. We had placed all the different cookies into their own tubs and had set them out on the kitchen counter.

All my worries had seemingly drifted away while making those cookies. It was almost therapeutic that Mom trusted me with making her world-famous Christmas cookies.

We headed down to our basement to play a board game while we waited for Amanda and Matt to arrive. We were about halfway through the game when Mom decided to order a couple of pizzas for the sleepover.

"The pizzas should arrive when Matt and Amanda get here. Should be about perfect timing," she said reassuringly. She took her seat at the table to take her next turn.

"I wonder if the *spooky elves* will come and get you and Amanda tonight," Colby said in his best creepy voice, waving his fingers to try to add to the effect.

I went to make a counterargument, but Dad threw his hand up and shook his head, silently telling me no as he spoke up.

"Colby, there will be none of that tonight. You understand?" he ordered while Mom moved her game piece on the board.

Colby sarcastically pouted, while Mom shouted in excitement because she had just landed on an important space that would likely help her win the game.

Our parents were just as competitive as Colby and me. Just because we were kids didn't mean they were going to let us win a board game.

"Ooh Hoo Hoo!" Mom taunted as she hopped out of her chair and started dancing. "You are all in trouble now!"

We all laughed at the ridiculous display Mom was putting on as we continued to finish playing the game.

There was a huge shift in her temperament minutes later when Dad wound up pulling out a game-winning move out of nowhere. She sat back in her chair, a look of disgust on her face as Dad flew out of his chair and started taunting all of us, making up his own terrible dance moves as he rubbed his victory in all our faces.

"Who's the best?" he asked after pausing his dance moves for a moment while, taking a second to look at each of us. "I'm the best! That's right! Uh-huh! Woo Hoo!"

All of us laughed some more. Dad didn't like to hold back his bragging in instances like this and we knew he would keep carrying it on as long as we stayed down here and allowed it. So slowly we each got up from our chairs to head upstairs since Matt and Amanda would arrive any moment now.

As we reached the top of the stairs, we could all hear Dad shout "Losers!" from down in the center of the basement. One last jab before we were out of earshot.

As we made our way through the living room and toward the kitchen, I couldn't help but look over at Alfie, Charlie, and Ernie perched up on the mantle overlooking our entire living room. I shuddered as I walked by. *I hate those stupid elves.*

Right on cue, as we reached the kitchen, we could see headlights pulling into the driveway as the sun had set and darkness had already fallen.

"Whoop whoop! Matt's here!" Colby called out excitedly as he slid into his slippers and burst out into the garage to go meet his friend.

"Oh, goodie," I muttered under my breath, eliciting a playful nudge from my mother.

I looked up at her and she mouthed the words, *Be nice.*

I nodded with a reluctant agreement, even though I knew the peace treaty would only last so long.

The two of them came storming into the house like they had just spent all day drinking nothing but caffeine. It was like watching a stampede of buffalo as they came bull-rushing into the house and the kitchen.

"What's up, Smellsy?" Matt cried sarcastically, grinning from ear to ear.

I turned to say something to him, but Mom cut me off again and suggested they both go upstairs and play some video games until the food was delivered.

They looked at each other and then, without warning, darted off and out of sight.

Mom had likely been bracing for this all day. It was usually a war when our friends stayed the night. I knew she was going to do her best to keep the peace in the house as long as she could. She merely looked down at me with a friendly shrug, knowing I wanted to say something.

"It'll be alright, Kelsey. Amanda should be here any minute," Mom said warmly as she walked over to the fridge and started getting out the two-liter bottles of soda for everyone.

She was right. Moments later, Amanda and her mom pulled into the driveway. They both came inside. My mom and Amanda's mom were nurses at the same hospital in Buffalo and were also good friends.

Mom frequently complained about the long drive to get to her job but always reminded us that the pay was much better up there, so she had to do it.

Amanda and I made our way into the living room. I proceeded to plug in the Christmas tree, and we turned on a movie. Dad marched through the living room and gave me one more victory gloat before making his way into the kitchen to hang out with Mom.

"So, what's new?" Amanda asked as we both kicked our footrests up.

The small talk felt weird, as we had just seen each other in school yesterday. I debated whether I should fill her in on the creepy elf dolls. I decided to keep it to myself. I'd had enough of my family looking at me like I was crazy for one day. I didn't need her piling it on.

I glanced up at the evil little elves on the mantle before looking back at Amanda. I frowned and replied with a "Nope, nothing at all."

I tried to ignore the feeling of being watched by them as we watched *Elf*.

Ironically.

13.

"Pizza's here!" Mom called out from the kitchen.

"Ooh! Perfect! I'm starving!" Amanda announced as she quickly ripped her blanket off and kicked her footrest down.

The smell of fresh pizza seeped through the house, and I felt my tummy growl like a ravenous dog as soon as that delicious scent filled my nostrils.

"Me too I guess!" I couldn't help but chuckle as I clutched my stomach.

I could hear Matt and Colby come bounding down the stairs. The herd was on its way through once again. I grabbed Amanda's arm and pulled her out of harm's way as Colby and Matt came barreling through the living room making racecar noises to show *how fast they were.*

"Outta the way, losers!" Colby sneered.

"Yeah, outta the way!" Matt repeated like an echo as they sprinted by us.

Amanda and I couldn't help but roll our eyes.

"Thanks," she said softly, shaking her head in annoyance.

"No problem. I have grown to learn over the last few years," I joked as we slowly started toward the kitchen.

"Oh, those are really cool!" Amanda commented, motioning toward the elves on the mantle. "Those new?"

I stopped in my tracks and hesitated for a second. "Yep, they're new," I muttered.

"What's wrong?" she inquired curiously.

"N-nothing. I just don't like them," I answered shortly as I began to start walking toward the kitchen again, trying to avoid talking about them.

"How do you not like friendly little elves?" Amanda called out as she followed behind my brisk pace toward the kitchen.

I pretended not to hear her as we made our way to the delicious-smelling food. Colby and Matt were already gathering their slices of pepperoni pizza and bringing them to the kitchen island to sit and eat. Mom brought each of them a glass filled with soda.

"Oh, it smells so good!" Amanda said, her eyes filled with a gluttonous hunger.

Mom and Dad merely smiled warmly as they handed each of us a slice of pie and had us sit on the last two stools at the kitchen island.

Mom handed each of us a glass of soda as well, and then she and Dad grabbed their own food and drinks. They conversed by the kitchen counters opposite us while we scoffed our food down like we hadn't eaten in weeks.

"Man, oh, man!" Colby said after polishing off his slice. "There's nothin' better than pizza."

"Agreed!" Matt said with his mouth full of his last bite.

They both hopped off their stools and went to the boxes of pizza to get another slice while Amanda and I continued to eat.

"So why don't you like the elves?" she asked again, curiously.

At this point, I knew she wasn't going to drop it.

"I'll tell you after we finish eating," I replied, hoping she would forget about it.

I really didn't want to have this conversation in front of everyone. I hoped that with her curiosity, *maybe* she would actually believe me.

We all lost our train of thought when Dad started doing his best Italian accent impersonation. He did this almost every time we ate Italian food.

"Oh, David, knock it off!" Mom said with a laugh and a friendly shove.

"Very funny, Mr. Carrow!" Matt said as he made his way back to the kitchen island to eat.

"Hey, thanks, Matt!" Dad said. He walked over and gave him a high five.

"Suck up," I couldn't help but say. It slipped.

"Whatever, Smellsy," Matt responded, eliciting laughter from himself and Colby.

"That's enough kids," Mom said, giving us a friendly warning as we all settled down and continued to eat.

No sooner had we finished dinner and started past the elf dolls, Amanda pressed me about them.

"Hold on," I told her, waving for her to follow me upstairs.

I broke one of my parents' rules and shut my bedroom door behind us. Amanda went and plopped down on my bed and eagerly awaited my answer to her question.

"So...what's going on?" she asked with a smirk.

I really didn't want to go into detail with her, fearing the worst. Knowing Amanda, however, she wasn't going to drop it now that she had her sights set on getting an answer from me.

I filled her in on the story, beginning with the flea market and Madame Trudeau. I told her what I'd seen the old woman doing at the store shortly before Mom came in and bought the dolls. I then went on to explain the strange occurrences that took place in the car, my hair getting pulled during the family photo, and the two times they'd somehow wound up in my room.

By the time I had finished filling her in, she had the same skeptical look on her face as my parents had earlier in the day.

"So...you're telling me you think they're *alive*?" Amanda asked with a hint of doubt.

"Yes! That's exactly what I am telling you!" I fired back. "You believe me, right?"

There was a moment of hesitation from Amanda before she responded. "Eh, I don't know, Kelsey. Are you sure it wasn't just some elaborate prank from Colby?"

"No! How do you explain my TV turning on by itself?" I argued frantically.

"Power surge?" she suggested with a shrug.

"Well, what about how they just randomly appeared on my bed this afternoon? Hmm?" I asked impatiently.

"Are you absolutely certain that Colby couldn't have just snuck in here while you were deep into your story and put them there?" Amanda questioned.

"No! I mean...I don't think so. Look, I don't know!" I replied, now doubting myself once again.

Amanda didn't believe me either, but was her thought process *really* all that farfetched? Could Colby have managed to sneak into my room while I was deep into the story? It was totally feasible. Could a power surge have turned my TV on? Again, it wasn't out of the realm of possibility. All of this could have been just one giant coincidence and could be connected to Colby getting better with his pranks.

"Look, I get it," Amanda said reassuringly. "I can see why you think they look creepy. But if I had to bet a week's worth of lunch money, I would bet that Colby has been pranking you."

I gave it some thought and agreed that she may be right. I started to feel a little bit better now, knowing that the dolls couldn't *actually* be alive.

14.

Amanda and I decided to turn on the TV and just hang out until a knock came at my door.

The door inched open as Dad poked his head into the room.

"You know the rules, no closed doors other than bedtime."

"Sorry, Dad," I replied.

"That's okay, honey. I came up here because Mom thought it would be fun for the two of you and the boys to play an old-fashioned game of hide and seek."

"Ugh! Dad, that sounds so lame!" I whined.

"I don't know, Kels, sounds like a fun time to me!" Amanda replied eagerly.

I shot a puzzled glance in her direction. "Really?" I asked in shock.

"Yeah, you guys have a big enough house, and there are Christmas decorations everywhere. I think it would be really fun!" Amanda beamed.

I couldn't help but shrug my shoulders, "Okay, hide and seek it is."

"Perfect! It's settled then!" Dad said gleefully as we made our way out of the bedroom.

"Well, what are you and Mom going to do?" I asked as we made our way down the staircase.

Dad let out a playful chuckle and mentioned that our neighbors across the street, the McNeil's, were going to be leaving on Monday to visit their family down in Pennsylvania for Christmas. So, they were going to head across the road and have a *few drinks* with them.

"Wait...so we're getting the whole place to ourselves?" I inquired.

"Well, for an hour or two anyhow, yes," Dad replied nonchalantly. "We will be right across the road and will have eyes on the house the whole time."

The McNeil's had a bar in their garage and my parents would hang out there every so often. We lived on the far outskirts of town, so there weren't many houses in our neighborhood. Traffic, or someone pulling up to our house, was the least of my concerns. It was more about what sort of chaos Colby could inflict even within a short amount of time.

"Sounds good, Dad," I replied modestly. "I know your cell number in case something should happen."

"I know you do, honey. You kids are starting to grow up. This will be a good test. We will give you all some time to play and have fun without us getting in the way. But as always, if you need anything don't hesitate to call."

"I won't, Dad," I replied, giving him a hug before meeting everyone else in the kitchen and hugging my mom as well before they took off.

"We will be back around 10. Don't break anything, be nice to each other, and most importantly, have fun!" Mom called out as Dad practically dragged her out of the house. They walked over to the McNeil's house.

I looked over at the clock. It was 8:23 PM. It wasn't a ton of time to have the house to ourselves. Certainly, there was enough time to play a game of hide and seek, and if need be, do a little mischief and get Colby back for his pranks.

"Alright! Home alone and some old-fashioned hide and seek," Colby announced with an excited head nod while rubbing his hands together. "Unless the big baby is too chicken."

"I'm not afraid. We'll do it," I challenged.

"Good, then you won't mind being the seeker, will you?" Colby dared.

"Ooh!" both Matt and shockingly, Amanda, responded at the same exact time.

"You're on!" I declared confidently. "How are we doing this?"

There was a slight pause. I could tell the wheels in Colby's head were spinning.

"Well, since we have the *whole house* to hide in, I feel like you should start in Mom and Dad's office and count to 60. That should be enough time for all of us to find a place to hide," he said this as if his brain was still working things out.

"Fine," I replied shortly. "Challenge accepted."

"Okay, well go to Mom and Dad's office. Don't start counting until you touch their desk," Colby ordered.

"Okay, fine," I replied as I made my way toward the office.

"No cheating!" I heard Amanda call out playfully. I heard their feet scampering lightly around behind me as I continued my trek into the room.

"I'm not going to cheat!" I yelled back with a chuckle and a little disbelief she'd said that.

My parents had an office because my dad said he was an *independent contractor* and was able to conduct business for his truck loads easier from there. The office also found other uses, like our family photos being edited.

The office wasn't very large. It was its own little section of the house, and very simplistic. Dad had a dark brown desk, with a monitor and keyboard resting on top, along with a couple of binders he used to keep track of business, and a container that he used to organize his pens, paper clips and other items. A red leather chair stood behind it.

The walls in the office were painted in a royal blue color. Dad's college degree in Business hung alongside his CDL certification. He also had different *Buffalo Bills* memorabilia hanging all over the walls as well. We were not allowed to mess with his stuff. His most prized possession was an autographed football helmet he'd had signed by several players on the team during their training camp a couple years ago.

I surveyed the room and took a deep, relaxing breath as I placed my hand on the desk and began to count.

"1...2...3..."

15.

I could hear frantic footsteps all throughout the house in all directions. It seemed like the footsteps had melded together before I heard someone go upstairs and into one of the bedrooms above me. I lost track of the other footsteps in all the commotion.

By the time I reached the count of 60, the house had fallen silent. Counting to 60 probably took me longer than a minute, but I don't think anyone was going to be upset by it.

"Ready or not...here I come!" I announced as loud as I could, slowly making my exit from my parents' office.

I decided to quickly make my way upstairs, as that was where I'd heard the footsteps.

Once I reached the top of the steps, I immediately went into Colby's room, thinking he may have gone in there. I checked everywhere, his closet, under his bed. Nobody was in Colby's room.

"They wouldn't dare," I whispered to myself as I marched from Colby's room down the hall to my room.

I took a quick glance under my bed, and it was empty except for some boxes I used to store old books, dolls, and clothes.

As I stood up, I froze. I heard what sounded like hoarse whispering coming from my closet. Multiple voices whispering back and forth to each other. I could feel my body tense up. I only heard one set of footsteps come up the stairs, but there were definitely three separate voices whispering in my closet, almost as if they were arguing with one another.

My heart raced as I slowly made my way to the closet. Everything fell dead silent once more. The only thing I could hear was my heart pounding, and my breathing becoming more rapid in the dark room.

I reached out to pull open the pull-out closet doors, and just I before I grabbed the knobs, the doors came bursting open. Screaming filled the house. I wasn't sure if it was my scream or what was going on. It was all a giant blur. All I know was that one of the elves appeared to have been floating in midair when the doors burst open.

I staggered backward and landed on the floor with a *thud*. By the time I crash-landed, laughter filled the room.

I quickly sat up in confusion as the light flicked on in my bedroom. I clutched at my chest, trying to calm down as I noticed Matt, Colby, *and* Amanda all in my room. Each of them was holding onto one of the elves.

Amanda quickly tossed her elf down and rushed over to help me up. I shot her a puzzled and betrayed glance.

"I'm sorry, Kels, they brought the idea up while you walked to the office, and I thought it would be funny. We shouldn't have done it," Amanda said apologetically while Matt and Colby continued their raucous laughter.

"I hate those stupid elves," I said through gritted teeth. I kicked Charlie the green elf, the one Amanda had tossed on the floor earlier.

Apparently, they had come up as a group and did their best to mask their footsteps, so it had sounded like only one person had come upstairs. They ensured that one person's footsteps stood out above the others.

"Oh, come on! It was just a prank!" Colby pleaded. "Fine, you all can hide this time, and I'll be the seeker. But no hiding together!"

"I'm done playing with you, Colby," I replied angrily as I got back to my feet. "And I can't believe *you* would team up with them like that." I shot Amanda a frustrated look, after dusting myself off.

"Look, we're sorry," Amanda reasoned. "It won't happen again. I promise."

I shook my head and let out a frustrated sigh.

"If it helps, I won't call you 'Smellsy' anymore," Matt tried bargaining. "If you play one more time."

I looked at each of them and saw the hopeful look in their eyes.

"No more funny business with the elves?" I asked.

"We swear," Colby said sternly. "And I'll be the seeker this time, so you know there will be no more funny business."

"Okay, fine," I groaned. "But if I get a hint at any more stunts like this, I'm done with you all for the night...that includes you, Amanda."

"Totally," Colby said as Matt and Amanda nodded their heads in agreement. Matt and Colby set their Jolly Elf dolls down on my desk.

"How long do you want me to count for? And where do you want me to start the count from?" Colby asked.

"Count to 100, but don't start until you get into your room and sit on the bed," I replied. "And close your eyes. No cheating, Colby."

Colby agreed to my request, and as he walked off toward his room, Matt and Amanda both veered off downstairs.

I heard Colby sit down on his bed and begin counting. I tried to scramble and think of a good place to hide.

I had a lightbulb moment go off in my head. If I could sneak into Colby's room and hide in *his closet* while he counted, he would never expect it!

Immediately, I crept out of my room. I peeked into Colby's room, and surprisingly, he was actually doing what I asked. He was sitting on his bed with his eyes closed. He had just reached the 30's in his count, so I had plenty of time.

I tiptoed across his room, being careful not to bump into anything. I reached his closet doors, and slowly drew them open.

I turned to look back at Colby, who still had his eyes closed and was now in the 40's. I couldn't help but smirk. I really wanted to laugh, knowing I was going to have him fooled, but I didn't want to ruin it.

I slowly climbed inside his closet, carefully prying his clothes apart just enough for me to squeeze in and not make any noise with his hangers.

I reached forward and shut the closet doors in total silence. I began to think I might be a ninja. I had never moved so stealthily in my life. Through the little slats in his closet doors, I could still see him sitting on his bed.

Finally, Colby reached the count of 100 and announced, "Ready or not, here I come!"

Predictably, he got up from his bed and immediately left his room, not bothering to check anywhere inside it.

"Yes!" I whispered gleefully to myself as I heard him creep down the bedroom hallway.

Things finally fell silent. I couldn't help but feel an exhilarating rush. A type of excitement that you only felt while hiding during a game of hide and seek.

Amidst all my elation, I heard a noise from my bedroom. Then another noise. Silence fell once more. Moments later, I heard a voice. A familiar voice.

Was Colby in my room playing with the elf dolls again? I could hear it plain as day now. There were three gravelly voices conversing in my bedroom.

"You aren't going to get me this time, Colby," I whispered to myself.

I slowly pushed open the closet doors again. Suddenly, winning the game didn't matter. If I could pull off a revenge prank and scare Colby, I was going to go for it.

I slowly crept back down the hall. My bedroom light remained on and covered a section of the hallway and walls, giving a slight illumination throughout the rest of the bedroom hallway.

As I drew nearer, the voices became clearer.

"These stupid kids," I heard one voice say.

"Yeah, can you believe the redheaded twit slammed me to the ground like that?" I heard another voice respond.

Something seemed different about these voices. It didn't *feel* like it was Colby saying these things.

I crept closer...and closer.

"Never worry. We'll teach them all a lesson they won't soon forget," the third voice added.

"You don't mess with elves," They all said in unison.

My heart absolutely stopped. There was *no way* Colby could speak three voices simultaneously like that. I froze dead in my tracks. I didn't know what to do.

I was completely on edge at this point. There was no way anyone else was upstairs. I decided I *needed* to know the answer.

I finally mustered up the courage to act. I decided not to creep forward anymore, and this time rushed into my bedroom and what I saw chilled me to my core. I didn't even know how to explain it.

As soon as I entered the room, all the elf dolls toppled over as if they had just gone rigid and came crashing down where they were previously standing.

I took a deep inhale of breath from shock before letting out another bone-chilling scream. *Were...were they alive?*

I covered my mouth as tears began to form in my eyes once again. I don't know if I caught them off guard or what. As soon as I entered the room, it was like they went limp and fell over. There was no one else upstairs and there were no more voices. It *had* to be them.

16.

Amanda, Colby, and Matt all came racing upstairs to see what was going on.

"How the heck did you get up here?" Colby asked in amazement as he came around the corner.

"What's wrong, Kelsey? Why did you scream?" Amanda asked as she ran up and gave me a comforting hug.

"The dolls. The dolls are alive!" I stammered. "I saw them move with my own eyes this time!"

"Oh, come on, Kelsey! Do you really think we are going to fall for that?" Colby asked with a tinge of insult in his voice. He shook his head.

"I'm not lying!" I pleaded desperately. "I thought you were in here messing around, Colby. I heard them talking!"

The three of them exchanged doubtful glances before Colby turned his attention back to me.

"Oh yeah? What did they say?" he challenged.

"I don't remember all of it. They sounded angry. They said they were going to teach us all a lesson, and not to mess with elves."

I turned toward the elves, who were all lying near each other.

"And then I came in here and *watched* them go stiff as a board and fall over."

I could tell they didn't believe me. This time I *knew* for certain that there was something very wrong with these elves.

"Sure thing, sis," Colby chastised. "You know, I was born at night, but I wasn't born *last* night."

"I am telling the truth! You believe me, don't you Amanda?" I turned and looked in her direction and watched her gaze fall to the floor.

"I don't know," she responded. "It does seem like an attempt at trying to get us all back."

Frustration began to build inside me at this point. *I'm not crazy.*

I turned my attention back to the ugly elves resting on my bedroom floor. I crouched down and violently yanked Ernie the white elf off the floor.

"Do something you stupid elf!" I exclaimed, shaking him around. "I know you can hear me!"

"Wow," Colby said shortly. "What a sad display."

Anger continued to swell as my desperation built. I tossed Ernie aside, sending him crashing into my dresser. I then reached down and picked up both Alfie the red elf and Charlie the green elf.

"Hey!" Colby cried out as he went to go check on Ernie.

"What? Are you guys too chicken to do anything because it's more than one person? Come on! I heard you talking! Do something!"

Again, the dolls remained silent. Their evil eyes and sinister smiles just eating away at me.

"Fine!" I growled as I slammed them both down. "I guess they are too afraid to do anything!"

"Or you could be lying," Matt said, inserting himself into the situation.

"You know what? Forget this!" I yelled as I turned and stormed out of the room. "Get your dumb elves out of my room and keep them out!"

"Kelsey!" I heard Amanda call out. I could hear her chasing behind me as I made my way down the staircase.

"Kelsey, slow down!" she yelled again. I could hear Matt and Colby laughing their heads off up in my room.

"I can't believe you don't think I'm telling the truth!" I said with watery eyes as I turned to her.

"I-I don't know what to say, Kelsey," she replied solemnly. "It is a pretty crazy thing to believe."

I took a deep breath. I could understand why she and everyone else would have a hard time believing me, but I *knew* what I just experienced. I didn't have any way to prove it though.

"I understand, Amanda. Let's just drop it, okay?" I replied, not knowing what else to do at this point. I couldn't *make* the elves come to life.

Amanda and I turned on a Christmas movie. Colby and Matt sounded like they'd returned to playing video games.

Mom and Dad made it home like clockwork, right at 10 like they said they would. Mom appeared to be both shocked and relieved the house was still in one piece while Dad seemed proud of all of us.

"So, who won hide and seek?" he asked enthusiastically.

Amanda and I shared a quick glance and said Colby won.

"Well, he is a crafty young man. You ladies will get him next time," he replied with a smile.

"Well, your father and I are going to go upstairs and relax. Thank you for not burning the house down. You kids have fun?" Mom asked as she and my dad began to head upstairs.

"I think we are going to sleep down here tonight," I hollered after them.

"That's fine, honey," Mom called out as they reached the top of the stairs and moved out of sight.

Amanda and I paused the movie while she went into the mudroom to grab her sleeping bag and get it set up. I was going to sleep on the couch.

"This is going to be so cool, sleeping next to the Christmas tree," she announced as she spread her sleeping bag out and flopped her pillow on the ground.

"Right!" I said to her as I sprawled out on the couch to get a little more comfortable. "I don't think I have ever slept down here with all the Christmas stuff out! It will be really neat!"

We both sat in silence with the TV paused as our eyes scanned the room. We took all the Christmas spirit in and shared a few lighthearted jokes before we started watching our movie again.

At some point, both Amanda and I wound up passing out with the TV still on.

17.

I don't know what caused me to stir awake in the middle of the night, whether it was the TV still on and the bright light randomly registering in my subconscious or what.

I just know I groggily awoke. I looked down at Amanda, who was lightly snoring, sleeping on her side with her back facing me.

I lethargically reached over to the end table above my head and grabbed the remote. I turned the TV off.

The Christmas tree lights illuminated the living room in a dim yet colorful holiday hue, splashing the room in a cascade of colors.

As I set the remote back down, I heard a rustling noise come from over by the tree. I quickly rose to a seated position on the couch. I frantically looked around at the tree but saw no movement. My breathing became very shallow as my whole body tensed up.

I didn't want to wake Amanda or anyone else up, so I remained still. I heard a clanking noise coming from our kitchen.

Could it have been the pipes clanging like they sometimes do in the wintertime?

I quickly and carefully got to my feet to inspect, being careful not to step on Amanda.

I crept toward the sound, entering the hallway between the living room and the kitchen. Suddenly, I heard a little *thud* back in the living room.

What in the world was going on? I felt like I was being pulled in multiple directions. I decided to go back to the sound in the living room. I retreated back to where I started, stopping at the opening of the living room.

Was I just hearing things? I know our senses are always heightened in the dark, but ever since I'd seen the elves earlier, I now felt like I needed to be on high alert.

I moved closer to the Christmas tree and knelt down. There was nothing there—other than some of the gifts that had already been wrapped.

Things fell silent in the house once more. I stood up and waited a few more moments in the dead silence. My eyelids were growing quite heavy.

"I must be half asleep still," I whispered to myself.

I slowly made my way back to the couch and threw the blanket over me. I heard the wind outside begin to howl and realized that houses always seem to make strange noises this time of year. I calmed down and, before I knew it, my eyes cemented shut as I dozed off. I thought I heard the faint sound of an evil laugh as I drifted off into a deep sleep.

18.

Just as the sun began to peer into the living room through our front window, I was abruptly awoken by a shrill scream coming from right next to me.

I immediately snapped awake, startled by the unexpected noise. I saw Amanda sitting on the ground next to me. In her hands were loose locks of her crimson hair.

Amanda immediately turned to me. Her eyes were filled with tears.

"What did you do?" she wept, aggressively waving strands of hair in my face.

"What did *I* do?" I asked, completely caught off guard as I sat up on the couch.

Before Amanda could answer me, I heard steps coming down the staircase. I looked over and saw a pair of scissors on the end table next to where my head had been resting moments ago.

"Was this because I didn't believe you about the elves?" she asked, her face turning a deep shade of red.

I didn't know what to say. I was in so much shock. Somehow, Amanda's hair had gotten chopped in the back, almost to her scalp, but leaving enough that it looked like she had a sideways mohawk now growing out of the back of her head.

"What's going on down here?" Dad yelled as he rushed into the living room and saw Amanda tightly clutching her locks of hair. "Oh...oh, no. What happened?"

"She cut my hair because I didn't believe those stupid elf dolls were alive!" Amanda accused, angrily pointing a rage-filled finger at me.

"I didn't do it! I swear!" I cried.

"Then why are the scissors right by the spot where you were sleeping? You didn't even have the decency to hide the evidence!" she shrieked. She got up, ran out of the living room in embarrassment and disappeared into our main floor bathroom, slamming the door behind her.

I couldn't even begin to wrap my mind around what was going on. I looked over and saw my parents along with Matt and Colby sharing troubled glances with one another. I don't think anyone knew what to say.

"Kelsey, how could you do that? She's your best friend," Mom asked finally.

"I didn't do it! Mom, I'm not lying! Why would I do that to my own friend?" I cried out.

"Because she helped us prank you last night," Colby muttered, squinting at me in an accusatory way.

"Is that what this is all about? A prank?" Dad demanded.

"How many times do I have to tell you I didn't do it?" I angrily fired back.

Normally, I wouldn't argue with my parents. If I was in the wrong, I would own up to it. I didn't cut Amanda's hair off and had no clue how it happened. My brain was going a mile a minute like a hamster in its wheel.

"Well, if you didn't do it...then who did?" Mom asked sarcastically.

Before I could even answer her question, I was cut off by Colby.

"Hey! What gives?" he yelled as he darted across the room toward the fireplace.

When I saw what he was looking at, my stomach turned.

Scribbled in what appeared to be permanent marker on his stocking, were several insults ranging from *Idiot* to *Bad Brother, Loser,* and even one which said: *A face only a mother could love.*

Everyone rushed over to look at the stocking while I still helplessly sat on the couch, feeling extremely uncomfortable.

Colby turned to look at me, his face was as red as the stocking he'd just turned away from.

"Why did you do that?" he asked with a shaky voice.

"Colby, I swear on everything...I didn't do that!" I replied, throwing up hands of surrender.

Before anyone could say anything else, I heard a deep gasp come from Mom.

"What's the matter, Sarah?" Dad asked. He looked down at what she was looking at on the floor. "Oh, no."

I got off the couch this time to see what was going on. When I saw what they were looking at, I couldn't believe it. My mom's favorite Christmas ornament, one that had been passed down from generation to generation starting with her grandma, lay on the floor shattered to pieces.

"Mom...I swear I di-..." I started to say. She cut me off by her waving a hand at me.

"N-not now, sweetie. Just give me a few minutes. Dave, will you take the kids into the kitchen and check on Amanda please?" she said, her voice filled with hurt.

"Sure, honey," Dad replied softly as he ushered us out of the room.

"Go wait in the kitchen, kids," he said with a disappointed wave as he walked over to the bathroom next to his office.

No sooner had we sat on the stools at the kitchen island, then Dad screamed out words that I am not allowed to repeat.

All of us immediately leaped out of our seats to see what was going on.

When we got to the office, we saw him standing in front of his once-autographed Buffalo Bills helmet. The case had been tossed aside, lying on the floor. Dad turned to us, holding onto his prized possession. It appeared that someone had scribbled all over it with the same sharpie that was used on Colby's stocking.

"Oh, Kelsey...no," I heard Colby whisper in fear.

I could see the absolute heartbreak in my father's eyes as he stared blankly at his helmet. He was speechless.

The rest of the morning was filled with absolute dread. It was one of the quietest mornings I could remember. I felt everyone shooting judgmental glances at me. Amanda wouldn't even look at me and had already called home for her parents to come pick her up.

I had tried to talk to her, but she wanted nothing to do with me. I don't know what happened, but *everything* came crumbling in on me all at once. It seemed that Matt and I were the only two that escaped having anything of ours being damaged, or so I thought.

When Matt's parents arrived to pick him up, he had come downstairs with his duffle bag filled with his stuff. It was absolutely soaked. Someone had dumped water all over his belongings.

I was now the only one who hadn't been messed with, which further made everyone cast agitated looks in my direction. I felt so isolated. So alone.

I ran upstairs after Matt and Amanda had left, bawling my eyes out. I quickly leapt onto my bed and cried furiously into my pillows.

Once I began to calm down, I rolled over and noticed the Jolly Elves sitting atop my dresser, with their backs resting against my TV, staring right at me.

I felt a wave of fear, anger, and utter disgust at the sight of them.

"It was you!" I said to the elves, still sobbing.

I jumped out of bed and marched over toward those ugly dolls. Right as I was about to swat them across the room, my mom came in.

"Hey, sweetie," she said in a sorrowful tone and a sniffle from her nose.

I quickly stopped what I was doing and turned to look at her. She came over and put an arm around me and guided me over to the bed where we sat together.

There was a long silence before she spoke.

"I'm sorry for the way everyone ganged up on you this morning. That wasn't right," she finally said with a deep exhale.

"Look...Mom..." I started to say before she began speaking again.

"All of those things are just that...*things*. Yes, they held sentimental value to all of us, but that didn't give us the right to react the way we did. It was obviously a cry out for help," she said while giving my shoulder a squeeze.

"I didn't do it though, Mom. I swear! I would never!" I replied hastily, wanting my voice to not only be heard, but understood.

Mom seemed to take it in stride. She took a deep breath.

"Then who do you think did?" Mom asked simply, glancing down at me.

"It's not a *who*, so much as a *what*," I told her as I looked over at the evil elves grinning at us from atop my dresser.

Mom seemed a little irritated by my continuing to blame the elves for all the bad things that had been happening. She threw her hands up in frustration and said she was done talking about the elves.

"They're just dolls!" she yelled in frustration as she exited the room, slamming my door behind her.

Obviously, she still didn't believe me. How could I blame her though?

After I'd had enough of looking at the three Jolly Elves, I took them over to Colby's bedroom and threw them on his bed.

"I hate you," I said to the motionless dolls as I left his room and shut the door behind me.

The rest of the day seemed to crawl by at a snail's pace until mid-afternoon when everyone's emotions seemed to return to somewhat normalcy.

Dad was down in the basement listening to music when Mom gathered Colby and me and said we were heading back to the flea market to get Colby a new stocking.

Then it dawned on me. I could ask Madame Trudeau what the heck was going on with these elf dolls!

19.

The drive back to the flea market was a quiet one. Mom had put on Christmas music, but none of us seemed to be in the spirit today.

I think Mom had partially decided to take us to the flea market to give Dad a little alone time. He hadn't really talked much since this morning.

"You should probably think about calling Amanda tomorrow and apologizing after she's had some time to cool down," Mom suggested as we turned down the main road and headed toward the flea market.

I didn't have any fight left in me at this point, so I replied with the short, sweet answer of, "I'll try."

The whole day had been a giant whirlwind. I began to think back to the menacing laugh I'd heard as I fell back to sleep. A cold shudder shook me to my core. I had to get to the bottom of this and I hoped Madame Trudeau would be able to help.

Mom pulled into the parking lot of the flea market. Predictably, it was packed. It was a sunny day on the weekend before Christmas.

We found a spot to park and made our way into the store with what appeared to be everyone else from the area. People were zooming back and forth between the booths as Christmas music blared over the store speakers. Toys were making noise, babies were crying, kids were running around. It was a madhouse.

"Do you want to go back to Madame Trudeau's store?" I offered.

Colby seemed to mull it over, "Sure. I think they could have some cool stockings."

Mom gripped onto both our hands as we worked our way through the sea of people and headed over to Madame Trudeau's. It appeared to be absolutely packed today.

I saw Madame Trudeau at the back of the store behind her counter, ringing up another family's items.

"H-Hey Mom, I'm just gonna head to the back of the store really quick," I said, tugging my hand free from her grip.

"Okay, just don't run off. We'll be over here with the stockings," she said as she motioned to the section of wall that held a variety of different stockings. "We shouldn't be too long."

I took the opportunity to rapidly make my way to the back of the store. I passed a kid blowing into an annoying kazoo as I weaved my way to Madame Trudeau's counter.

She glanced down at me with a friendly smile.

"Can I help you?" she asked in her sweetest voice.

"Yeah, uh…I don't know if you remember me or not. I got a snow globe from here and my brother got some elf dolls," I said awkwardly.

"Oh, yes!" the old lady beamed. "How are you enjoying the decorations?"

"Well, see that's the thing. There's something wrong with those elves," I said.

A puzzled look formed across her face, as she straightened her glasses.

"Oh? How so?" she inquired, lips pursed and a concerned look on her face. She leaned over the counter so she could hear better.

"Okay, this is going to sound crazy, but I think the elf dolls are alive!" I told her desperately.

To my shock, she started laughing.

"Oh, honey. That's a good one! I needed that laugh. Thank you!" Madame Trudeau bellowed.

"I'm telling the truth!" I replied earnestly. "And I saw you do some weird ritual above them the night we bought them."

Madame Trudeau's face went from a jolly expression to a stern glare as she straightened her glasses once more.

Before either of us could say anything else, I felt someone standing behind me. I glanced back and saw my mom angrily staring down at me.

"Again, with these dolls," she growled. "I'm so sorry. You'll have to excuse her."

"Oh, it's quite alright dear," replied Madame Trudeau.

"Go wait by the exit," Mom ordered as she and Colby handed Madame Trudeau the stocking he had picked out.

"But Mom, I saw her doing some weird stuff over the dolls right before we bought them!" I tried reasoning.

"Kelsey, I am not going to tell you twice," she replied sternly and pointed toward the exit of the store.

I begrudgingly stomped forward. I could hear my mom apologizing to Madame Trudeau. My blood was boiling. My hope for help had quickly dimmed and disappeared. I was back to being on my own once again.

I glanced back to the counter one last time and saw Madame Trudeau shoot me a wicked grin before turning her sights back to Mom and Colby with her normal, warm smile.

I felt a knot in the pit of my stomach. I felt sick. She did this, and I didn't have a clue what to do or how to stop it. My whole world had been flipped upside down over the last couple days, and my Christmas spirit had diminished.

I stood at the entrance, looking out at all the excited faces and happy families. I yearned to have that back again.

I now knew deep down that Madame Trudeau had caused this, but for the life of me, I didn't know why. *Why would she do this? Why would she ruin our Christmas? What did she have against us? And how did she make the elves come to life? Was it all a ploy to tear apart a family at a time that is meant to be happy? Did she just flat out hate Christmas?*

I had all these thoughts running through my head as Mom and Colby came storming out of the store. Mom gripped my hand and led us back to the car once again.

"Thank you for the new stocking, Mom. It's really neat!" Colby exclaimed as he held up his red and green striped stocking.

"You're welcome, honey," she said in a loving voice.

"Mom, I know you're tired of hearing me say this, but I swear something is going on with those..." Before I could finish my sentence, Mom abruptly cut me off in frustration.

"If I have to hear about those elves being alive one more time, Kelsey, I am going to lose my temper," she threatened.

"But, Mom!" I bellowed.

"That's it! The elf dolls are getting put away until next Christmas," Mom said scornfully, shaking her head as her voice wavered with anger.

"That's not fair, Mom!" Colby cried out.

"I'm sorry, Colby. I think it is for the best right now," she replied bluntly.

Colby looked over at me with disgust. "Thanks a lot, Kelsey."

I couldn't even muster a response to Colby at this point. I felt like the world's largest villain. Was I *actually* going crazy? Did I *actually* do all these things to everyone and not realize it? Was I just making things up in my mind about Madame Trudeau and these elves?

I just couldn't get my brain to wrap around anything going on anymore. I didn't know what was up, what was down, or what was left or right at this point.

The remainder of the car ride was a quiet one as I stared out the window deep in my own thoughts. I was hopeful that putting the elf dolls away would solve all our problems.

20.

When we arrived home, Dad was busily making one of his favorite dishes, country fried steak with mashed potatoes. My stomach grumbled wildly as soon as the smell hit my nose.

He seemed to be in better spirits when we all came walking into the kitchen. I wasn't sure if it was because he'd had a little alone time, or the food, but he was humming along to the rock song he had playing through our Bluetooth speaker. He seemed to be excited at our arrival.

"What is up Carrow fam?" he asked enthusiastically as he bobbed his head to the song.

"Honey...is everything okay?" Mom asked curiously.

I think she was just as confused as me and Colby.

"Yeah, everything is great!" he exclaimed as he vigorously stirred the mashed potatoes.

The three of us exchanged bewildered glances. Colby shrugged as he and I both hopped up to sit at the kitchen island.

"Well, that's certainly a change of heart from this morning," Mom replied with a smile.

Dad set the pan down and turned to look at all of us. "Yeah, you know what? I came to the realization that *things*...items don't matter. What matters most is spending time with family."

"I couldn't have said it better myself," Mom agreed.

"With that being said," Dad said with a pause. "I do have to head out to Oklahoma for a delivery tomorrow morning, but I will be back on Christmas Eve."

Mom gave Dad a look of disapproval, "David, this close to the holiday?"

"Unfortunately, I couldn't say no," he said with a brief hesitation. "They offered me triple my rate, and I will still be home for the holiday."

I could tell Mom was a little upset by this news but tried her best not to show it. This was the type of thing that Dad always reinforced to me and Colby about hard work and making sure we were taken care of.

"I know it isn't the greatest news," Dad continued. "But I will make it up to everyone. I promise."

Dad walked over and gave Mom a kiss on the forehead. Of course, me and Colby had to make noises as if we were grossed out. They both chuckled. Dad went back to prepping dinner, and Mom turned to us.

"Come on. Time to put the elves away," she declared.

"Oh, come on Mom, do we have to?" Colby tried to reason.

"Yep. We are done with the elves for this year," she said sternly.

Dad turned as if he was going to say something but quietly decided to go back to cooking.

I couldn't help but feel elation knowing we were finally about to lock those evil little things away. I told Mom that I had placed them on Colby's bed. She went into the hallway closet and grabbed an old shoebox as we made our way upstairs. Colby was still pleading his case, but Mom wasn't having it.

When we reached Colby's room, Mom stopped at the doorway.

"Huh," she said, fiddling her fingers at the box, "That's weird."

"What's going on?" Colby demanded as he squeezed around Mom and into his room. "Where are they?"

"They aren't in there?" I asked in a shocked tone, my stomach beginning to turn.

"No," Mom said in bewilderment. "Honey, did you move them?" she asked.

"No," I replied anxiously. Something didn't feel right. "I distinctly remember putting them on his bed."

"Well, they didn't just up and walk away," Mom answered shrewdly. "Maybe your father moved them."

She set the box down on my bed and marched downstairs to see if Dad had moved them. I slowly made my way into my room with Colby close behind. Colby made himself right at home and began searching through my closet to see if I had hidden his precious dolls.

"I didn't hide them, Colby," I growled.

"Yeah, you're probably right," he said with a breath of arrogance. "You've been jealous ever since I got them. That's why you've been doing all this stuff."

Before I could fire back a response, Mom came back clutching the little devils themselves in her arms.

"See, I told you!" I yelled at Colby.

"Yeah. Yeah," he replied nonchalantly.

"Apparently, your father moved them downstairs and put them on the TV stand," she said as she made her way toward the box on my bed.

I couldn't help but think, *at least they didn't up and walk there themselves.*

Mom grabbed the shoe box out of Colby's room. She came in, pulled the lid off the box and placed the three elves inside it. Just as Mom was putting the lid down, I thought I saw a grimace of absolute fury on Alfie's face. Mom let out a sigh of relief as she quickly scooped the box up and exited the room.

Colby and I followed close behind. We watched as Mom put the box up on the top shelf in the closet downstairs where we couldn't reach it without the help of a step ladder.

"There! No more elves. We are done with them for this year," she said gleefully.

A little later, we sat down as a family and had dinner. Things seemed to be back to normal. After dinner, Dad began getting things ready for his trip to Oklahoma in the morning. He had to be up super early. He mentioned having to head out around 4:00 AM to get a head start on things. We were all going to miss him greatly, but he had his *talk* with us like usual before he got ready to leave.

Colby, Mom, and I played a couple of board games while he got ready, and we all closed the night out on a high note by watching *A Christmas Story* before going to bed.

The day's events had worn me down, and I was so excited to get a full night's sleep for once.

21.

For some reason, I found sleep was difficult to find on this night. I tossed and turned. I couldn't get comfortable, and when I did fall asleep, I found myself having nightmares about the elf dolls running amok through the house and tearing up even more stuff.

I looked over at my computer to look at the time. It was 1:42 AM. I let out a frustrated groan. All I wanted was one solid night's rest, but something just wasn't sitting right in the pit of my stomach. It *still* felt like something was off.

For some reason as I lay alone in my room shrouded in darkness, my gut told me I wasn't alone. I tried my best to clear my mind to fall asleep. I tried counting back from 100. I tried closing my eyes and picturing Christmas morning with my family all in good spirits. Nothing I tried could shake the feeling I had.

I pounded on my bed with frustrated fists. "I just want to sleep," I whispered to myself.

Agonizing minute after agonizing minute passed by. Having not gotten a full night's rest in several days, I was at my breaking point.

I decided to get up and try to go to the bathroom. I quietly tiptoed across my room and opened the door. The house was completely still. I carefully made my way to the end of the hall and entered the bathroom.

The fact that things seemed and felt normal out in the hallway had comforted me a touch. I began to feel better as I finished using the restroom.

I went back to my room, shut the door behind me, and crawled back into bed. Sometimes just getting up and then coming back to bed has helped me fall asleep before. This time seemed no different.

My heavy eyelids finally seemed to find pay dirt as I found a comfy position and dozed off.

Just like the nightmarish evening when Amanda had stayed the night, I heard a sinister laugh as my deep sleep started kicking in.

Somewhere in the depths of my slumber, I could hear voices. Faint voices in the distance.

I could hear the whispers slowly becoming clearer.

"So, they think stuffing us in a box will keep us at bay," one voice said.

"They got another thing comin,'" another voice whispered.

"Let's have some fun," a third voice whispered, this one sounding *even closer*.

I stirred in my sleep a little as I rolled onto my side. I don't know why, but somewhere in my deep state of sleep I could feel my heart racing.

"Hey, you...Wake up," a callous, whispery voice hissed seemingly right in front of my face.

"I said wake up!" the voice called out again, this time howling in a much louder and more menacing voice.

I immediately jolted awake. Standing directly in front of my face with the meanest scowl I had ever seen, was Alfie the red elf.

My eyes grew wide. I wanted to scream, but I think the sheer confusion, panic, and pure fear of what I was witnessing at that moment kept it stuffed deep down inside me.

"Thanks for joining us, sleeping beauty!" another voice called from right above my head.

I instinctively rolled onto my back to look, and standing on my pillow directly above my head was Charlie the green elf. He too had an evil look spread across his face.

I was in a total state of disbelief. I wasn't sure if it was possible to be scared to death, but I had to be close to it at this point. I had never felt such dread in my entire life. I was frozen with fear and my heart felt like it was going to burst through my chest at any moment.

Suddenly, I felt the blanket get tossed aside at the foot of the bed.

"Tickle, tickle," called a third voice from down by my feet.

It was Ernie, the white elf. He began to rake his cold rubbery fingers across the soles of my feet. I immediately yanked them away, and just as I was about to scream to alert my parents, Alfie crammed one of my dirty socks into my mouth with surprising strength. He silenced the scream.

I was taken aback by this move, and immediately the three elves pounced on me with such speed and force, I barely had time to react.

"You think you can lock us away?" Alfie called out menacingly as he began crawling on my face.

"We'll show you!" called out Charlie.

I immediately jumped up in my bed springing into action. I didn't know what these little dolls wanted from me, or why they were attacking me, but I quickly went on the offensive. I grabbed Alfie off my face, throwing him across the room. He crashed into my dresser and fell to the floor with a light *thud*.

Charlie and Ernie kept hopping around, laughing and giggling at my predicament. Finally, I managed to swat Charlie off and he bounced off my computer monitor and out of sight. That left just Ernie, the elder elf of the trio. He proceeded to bite my ankle, sending a surge of pain that felt like a bee sting soaring through my leg.

I wailed into the sock that had been crammed into my mouth, and flailed my leg as hard as I could, sending the little elf flying off my bed and out of sight.

Things fell silent in my room. I quickly spit the disgusting sock out of my mouth and looked at my ankle which was throbbing with a stinging pain. With the little bit of moonlight peering through my window, I could see what appeared to be a red circle welting up on my skin.

With sweat now pouring out of me, and my stomach tied in several knots, I needed to know if the elves were done for the night. I slowly scooted myself toward the foot of my bed to see if any of them were lying where I had just tossed and smacked them.

To my utter horror and shock, neither Ernie nor Alfie were resting where I had flung them. I quickly pivoted toward my computer desk. Charlie was also gone.

That meant they were still alive and well. It meant they could only be hiding in one place. I felt like I was about to hyperventilate. Up to this point, it was only suspicion and paranoia in my head that the elves were alive, but I had never actually seen them move and talk until now. All my worst fears had finally come to the forefront, and I was scared out of my mind.

I scooched over toward my nightstand and opened my drawer. Reaching in, I quickly grabbed my little flashlight.

Dad had always taught Colby and me to keep one in our nightstands in case we ever lost power.

Part of me wanted to yell for help, but every time I had done that up to this point, it had only gotten me into more trouble. I knew the elves would likely go stiff again. Part of me wanted to run away from my room as fast as possible, but I knew that wouldn't solve anything either.

I decided I needed to see what was going on. I clicked my flashlight on, and slowly leaned over the side of my bed so I could shine my light under and see if I could find the elves.

Just as I peeked my head under my bed, my flashlight began to flicker.

"No. No. No!" I hissed, smacking the flashlight against the palm of my hand.

I finally got the flashlight to kick back on. I turned it around and swept it around beneath my mattress. I scanned the light back and forth, trying to see any sort of movement between all the boxes I had slid underneath.

Suddenly, there was a gravelly yell, and a flurry of colors flew out at me. Before I could react, they dragged my unbalanced body off my bed, sending me toppling to the floor with a hard crash.

This time I let out an ear-piercing scream that reverberated through the entire house. Just mere seconds later, I heard footsteps rushing toward my room. My door flew open, and my light immediately flicked on.

I looked up and saw the worried look on both my parents' faces. It looked like they were about to speak and then stopped themselves.

I looked down at the ground next to me. The elf dolls had gone stiff as a board once more and lay around me like autumn leaves on the forest floor.

"What are those dolls doing up here?" Mom asked furiously. Colby slowly peeked into my room, squeezing his face between Mom and the doorframe to see what was going on.

"They came up here and attacked me!" I sobbed, leaping to my feet. I ran over and gave them both hugs.

"Kelsey, I have to be up in two hours for work. We decided to put these elves away to stop these pranks from happening," Dad responded in frustration.

I took a step back, wiping the tears from my eyes. "You guys *still* don't believe me? Look at my ankle!"

I lifted my ankle up to show them the red circle that had formed on my ankle bone from Ernie biting me just moments ago.

I looked up and saw them exchange worried glances. Silence fell upon my room. I could tell they were troubled to see the mark on my ankle but still weren't buying the story I was telling them.

My whole world felt like it had been flipped upside down. I felt like I was living in my own personal horror movie during a time that was supposed to be the happiest of the year for our family.

It felt like a divide was beginning to happen. I hated everything that was going on. Most of all I hated those elves.

Mom and Dad told Colby to go back to bed, and then they stepped out into the hallway, shutting my door behind them. They appeared to be having a discussion.

Moments later, Mom hastily made her way over to the dolls and scooped them up.

"We are going to put an end to this once and for all," she warned as she rushed past me and out of my room.

She and my dad rushed down the staircase. I chased after them.

"You guys *still* don't believe me?" I cried out. "Even after showing you what they did to my ankle? They even dragged me out of bed!"

I couldn't believe what was going on. My parents had always given Colby and me the benefit of the doubt, even when we didn't deserve it. Now, in one of the most frightening times of my life, when I needed their belief and support the most, they weren't having it.

"We don't know what to believe, Kelsey," she replied as we reached the closet where the elves were previously stowed away.

The sliding closet door was wide open, and the shoe box lay on the floor with the lid off to the side.

"See!" I urged. "No step ladder anywhere in sight. I couldn't have gotten them down."

"Enough, Kelsey," Mom replied sternly.

In the meantime, Dad continued through the kitchen and out to our garage. He returned moments later with a roll of duct tape.

Quickly and efficiently, Mom and Dad worked together. Mom stuffed the dolls inside the shoe box and held it up while Dad wound the duct tape around it several times at the top, middle, and bottom of the shoe box.

They then returned the shoe box to its spot atop the shelf in the closet before sliding the door shut once more.

"Now...we are going to go back to sleep. No more of this elf nonsense," Mom ordered.

I knew there was no point in me trying to argue anymore. Clearly, the idea of the elf dolls coming to life was something they just couldn't understand or believe no matter how hard I pleaded or wished they would.

We marched upstairs, and even though my parents were angry with me, they each gave me a hug and a kiss on my forehead.

"I hate that we are being so hard on you, honey. We love you and just want you to enjoy Christmas and stop with the pranks," Mom said as she tucked me into my bed.

I merely nodded my head, my eyes still watering at the isolated feeling I had.

"Get some sleep," Mom said softly as she turned my light off and shut my door.

I felt like it would be a miracle if I fell asleep at this point. If nobody would believe that I was just attacked when I had a physical mark to prove it, then I might truly be in this battle all alone, and that was just as frightening as the elves themselves.

22.

After last night's fiasco, I had, at some point, managed to fall asleep. The unforgiving sun, however, peeked through my bedroom window once I finally felt as though I'd started to get some decent sleep.

I groggily yawned awake, sat up and stretched. My body felt like it had been hit by a truck. My back was sore, and my ankle was still a little achy.

I rolled out of bed and headed downstairs. I made my way to the kitchen where I saw my mom, in her bathrobe, sitting at the kitchen island sipping on her morning coffee and scrolling through her tablet.

She glanced over when she saw me walk into the kitchen and greeted me with a warmer smile than I'd anticipated.

"Good morning," she said in her normal motherly tone.

"Good morning," I replied bashfully.

"I'm sorry about how last night was handled," she admitted as she took another sip from her coffee mug and patted the stool next to her.

Unsure of how to respond, I said nothing and took a seat next to her.

We had a short conversation, mostly about how she wanted us to be a normal family again and to get back to enjoying Christmas time and hoped we could all get past the events that had taken place over the last few days.

"You want some cereal?" she asked as she sorted through our cupboards.

"Sure," I replied timidly.

I couldn't shake the feeling of shame and abandonment in this situation. I know she felt bad and wanted to believe me deep down but just couldn't bring herself to accept my story about the elf dolls coming to life.

She poured a bowl of cereal and brought it over. Then, she sat next to me once more.

"I was thinking maybe we could head over to Lake Chautauqua today, maybe go sledding. Something fun, you know?" she suggested.

The sentiment made me feel better.

"Sure, that would be fun!" I replied.

I had always enjoyed sled riding for as long as I could remember. It was one of the few times that Colby and I didn't argue and would just have a blast racing down a snowy hill.

"Maybe try calling Amanda and see if she would want to come?" Mom offered with a hopeful gleam in her eyes.

"Mom, I don't think she is going to want to talk to me," I replied with a heavy heart.

"Well, as your father always says, *you won't know if you don't try,*" she said in her best Dad impression.

I merely nodded as I started eating my cereal, but cracked a smile at Mom's silly attempt at lifting my spirits.

Not long after I finished eating my cereal, Colby came wandering into the kitchen like a zombie. His hair was a mess, and his eyes looked baggy.

I think the events of the last few nights with me screaming in the middle of the night was messing with his sleep as well.

Mom informed Colby of today's plans, and he seemed eager for a fun-filled day as well.

She offered Colby a bowl of cereal, which he gratefully scoffed down like a wild hog. We were all cracking jokes with one another, and the energy in the house seemed to be uplifting finally.

After breakfast, Mom told us to see if our friends wanted to come with us. She handed her cell phone over to Colby. He called Matt to see if he could go sledding with us, but apparently, he was with his grandparents over an hour away since his parents were working and said he wouldn't be able to go.

I was up next. I dialed Amanda's cell phone number which she promptly picked up. I wanted a little privacy, so I walked out of the kitchen and into my parents' office. I opened the conversation by apologizing to Amanda about what happened to her hair. She seemed grateful for my apology.

I immediately filled her in on what happened last night with the elves attacking me. She seemed annoyed and apprehensive at first and was asking a lot of questions. I could tell that a small part of Amanda still didn't believe me even though she said she did. I told her my parents had essentially locked the elf dolls away in a box sealed with duct tape and that, hopefully, the nightmare was over.

After a few more minutes, Amanda wound up apologizing for not believing me.

"I knew you wouldn't have done that to my hair," she confessed.

It felt so good to finally have someone believe me with what was going on. Finally, I managed to invite her to come with me, Colby, and Mom for a fun day.

She seemed uneasy at first, but said if her mom was okay with it, she was in.

I was so excited when we got off the phone, I couldn't wait to tell Mom the good news. She seemed relieved that Amanda was so quick to forgive me for everything that had happened and that my best friend was willing to hang out so soon.

"Alright, well let's get ready and we will go pick her up," Mom announced. "Go get changed and we will head out!"

Colby and I rushed out of the room and changed into our snow outfits. I put on my navy blue snow pants, pink coat, and my pink and grey striped beanie to keep my head warm.

Colby came down dressed in his black snow pants, white coat, and black beanie cap.

Mom greeted us at the bottom of the stairs in her normal snow attire. She had on a pair of lime green snow pants, her white snow coat, and a white hat.

"Looks like we are ready to rock!" she said. We all made our way out to the garage and headed out to pick up Amanda on our way to Lake Chautauqua.

23.

Lake Chautauqua was a beautiful place not more than a 15-minute drive from our home. There was an infamous place called Glenview Hill where many kids from the area would go sledding. It had a steep slope where you could really get some fantastic speed. And from the top, you could see Lake Chautauqua in all its glory.

It was so neat that our mom was able to take a vacation this entire week. It meant we could go out and do fun stuff during the day, not just after she got home from work. Normally, we would be sequestered inside all day until she got home.

We had finally picked Amanda up from her house. Luckily with it being winter, her beanie hat was covering what happened to her hair, so you couldn't even tell what had happened. That gave me a little relief.

As we were on our way to Glenview Hill, a special weather alert announcement came through on the radio.

It warned about a possible winter storm watch that would be in effect and heading our way on Christmas Eve. The weatherman said we could be looking at anywhere from 12 to 16 inches of snow on Christmas Eve—starting in the morning.

"Oh, great!" Mom grumbled.

"What? That should be really neat!" Amanda exclaimed.

"If storms get bad enough, they'll call me into work beforehand knowing the increased likelihood of bad car accidents," Mom replied, her voice filled with dread.

Being in western New York, we frequently got really bad snowstorms from the weather that blew across Lake Erie. There was a time, a couple years ago, when we had gotten over four feet of snow. We hadn't gone to school for almost a whole week!

Mom was right though, if this storm actually did become more likely, the hospital would very likely call her into work during the heart of it, in case of an outbreak of car crashes.

As cool as it would be to have a big snowstorm on Christmas Eve, I was hopeful the heaviest parts would miss us. Dad was supposed to be coming home on Christmas Eve, and Mom was supposed to be off work. Could anything else go wrong on this winter break?

We finally made it to Glenview Hill, and it was packed. Kids were flying down the hill on their sleds and tubes at high rates of speed. Laughs and screams filled the park. It was a perfect day for sledding. With overcast skies and light flurries of snow flickering to the ground, we quickly marched to the top of the hill with our sleds in hand.

Mom decided to hang out with the other parents down in the parking lot, watching their kids slosh down the slope and then struggle to make their way back up the steep hill.

We noticed that a group of kids had built a ramp out of the snow, and Colby convinced us that we all needed to try it.

"No way, Colby," I said defensively.

"What are you? Chicken?" he said as he began imitating a chicken and making clucking noises.

Oh, joy, the age-old insult that *always* worked and never went out of style.

"Fine, I'm in," I declared as we continued over the top of the hill to the line waiting to go down the hill and hit the ramp.

Colby ran as fast as his legs would allow him in the ankle-deep snow.

"So," Amanda spoke with a pause. "The elf dolls are real, huh?"

I was taken aback that she wanted to bring it up. I looked over and nodded as we passed a group of kids arguing about whether they should go down the hill.

"Do you think them being in a box that is taped shut will keep them in there for good?" she asked, a hint of worry in her voice.

"I hope so," I replied as we met up with Colby and waited in line.

I hadn't really thought about it much. *Could* the duct-taped box hold them? I knew from experience that the elves were much stronger than their small demeanor would indicate. However, I didn't see a way for them to get out of the box. I felt good overall, the more I thought about it.

"Looks like I'm up," Colby said, his voice shaky.

"Well, go on then!" I called out to him. "What are you? Chicken?" I taunted, doing my own mimic of a chicken now.

"Shut up!" he yelled. "If you're so tough, you go down first!"

"Okay, fine," I replied, accepting the challenge.

At this point, anything to one-up him and shut him up for a day was worth any potential injury.

Before Colby could say a word, I went running past him, flopped down onto my stomach and slid down the hill with a running start, aimed straight for the ramp near the bottom of the hill.

I felt an exhilarating rush as I continued to pick up speed, the cold wind whipping against my face, and little flakes of snow falling all around me. I couldn't help but let out an excited yell and laugh hysterically at the same time. It was such a rush!

It felt like everything slowed down, even though I knew I was flying down the hill. The ramp was drawing closer, and my heart began pumping faster and faster. I began to brace myself for the oncoming flight I was about to experience.

Shoom! I glided right over the top of the ramp and went airborne. It felt like I was in the air for an eternity, and my stomach flew up into my chest as I came crashing back down to Earth with a hard *thud*. My sled continued to plow forward for a bit before coming to a screeching halt.

I hopped off my sled and threw both arms in the air as I turned and looked back up to the top of the hill in triumphant victory.

Not long after, Amanda came flying down as well. Eventually Colby, not to be outdone, came down after Amanda and met us both at the bottom of the hill.

"That...was awesome!" he yelled.

We went back up and down the hill several times, having the time of our lives. Sometimes we opted to just go straight down the hill instead of waiting in line for the ramp.

We even managed to convince Mom to sled down the hill just once. She let out a scream that sounded eerily similar to me when I saw the elves, as she glided down the hill at a high speed, before barrel-rolling out of the sled at the bottom of the hill. We could hear her laughing hysterically.

I guess sometimes it's good to feel like a kid again.

24.

The sun began to set as we headed back toward Jamestown. We stopped at a fast-food restaurant outside of town, and Mom suggested we go to downtown Jamestown to see the lights and the giant Christmas tree in the town center before we took Amanda home.

As night fell, we parked in the town square to walk around and take in the sights of downtown Jamestown. The snow flurries had begun to grow into larger flakes but fluttered softly to the ground in a very tranquil way and didn't appear to be sticking to the roads.

Jamestown always did a terrific job showing the Christmas spirit. All the businesses downtown were lit up, wreaths hung from all the lamp posts that lined the sidewalks. In the middle of town, we finally saw the town's Christmas tree in all its glory. It stood at least 30 feet tall, and was decorated to the brim with different ornaments, multi-colored lights, and garland. The tree topper was a giant star that cycled through different colors. Next to the tree, was Santa's sleigh. It sat idly by with decorative reindeer standing at the helm.

"This never gets old," Mom said with a sparkle in her eyes.

We were all in agreement, exchanging our oohs and ahs along with the other families downtown taking in the sights. All the events of the past few days began to melt away from my memory. I was feeling better.

Everyone's spirits seemed to be in high order as we dropped Amanada off and got home. Even the tension in our house seemed to have melted away and returned to normal. We turned on all the Christmas lights and decorations throughout the house, played a board game, and watched a Christmas movie before heading off to bed.

I remembered feeling a tinge of anxiety as I rolled into bed. My mind drifted to the *what if*.

I fell asleep and the next thing I knew, it was morning. I looked over at my computer and saw it was 8:49 AM. I'd had a full night's sleep! I was so excited. I quickly hopped out of bed. Ironically, I felt as excited as I would getting up on Christmas morning. The elves were trapped or gave up. One or the other. Either way, things appeared to be back to normal.

The whole day went smoothly. We were drawing nearer to Christmas, and my excitement was growing. Mom had left for a bit to finish up her Christmas shopping *with the crazies* as she always liked to say. I spent most of the day reading while Colby played his video games.

The only thing looming that could ruin my spirits right now, were all the news alerts about the upcoming snowstorm. It was becoming more and more likely the storm would strike the area on Christmas Eve. I was extremely hopeful that Colby and I wouldn't be locked in the house all day on Christmas Eve without either of our parents.

My excitement the next morning waking up with back-to-back nights of getting uninterrupted sleep was quickly ruined when I headed down to the kitchen and overheard my mom talking on the phone.

I could tell from the conversation that her work was calling her to inform her she was going to have to come in on Christmas Eve.

As Mom hung up the call, she seemed a little distraught. When she noticed me standing in the doorway to the kitchen, she appeared to hide it as best she could.

"Oh, hey, honey," she said in a woeful tone.

"Have to go into work tomorrow?" I asked, trying not to sound upset.

"Unfortunately, I do," she replied with a sigh. "Hopefully, since the weather alerts have been going off like crazy and with it being a holiday, most people will stay home, and I'll be able to get off early. I'm so sorry, honey."

"It's okay, Mom. I get it. You have an important job," I answered reassuringly.

And what I'd said was true. I'd learned over the last couple years just how important both of my parents' jobs were. Without truck drivers like my dad, people wouldn't have a lot of the things they do. And without nurses like my mom, we wouldn't have people who could take care of us when we were sick or hurt.

"I promise, I will make it up to you both," she said as she came up and hugged me.

"It's okay, Mom. Really," I said, giving her a big squeeze in return.

"Now run along upstairs," she ordered. "I need to finish wrapping yours and Colby's gifts. Tell him to stay upstairs too."

I did as I was told and quickly ran upstairs. Colby was busily mashing the buttons on his controller. He nonchalantly acknowledged what I said and went back to playing his game.

I was close to finishing my book, so I thought this would be a good time to try to wrap it up.

I plopped down on my bed once again, feeling a little let down by the fact that my parents were going to be gone most of the day on Christmas Eve. I just hoped with the weather, both would be home safely and in time for Christmas Day at this point.

25.

The next morning, Mom woke both Colby and me up early as she was getting ready to leave for work. I looked out my window and the snow had already begun to fall heavily.

"I've already made you sandwiches for lunch," Mom said as she hurried down the staircase, hollering back toward us. "Feel free to pour yourselves bowls of cereal for breakfast. I'm hoping to be back by late afternoon or early evening."

I noticed, as we made our way into the living room, that beneath the tree, a lot more presents had been wrapped and placed underneath since yesterday. Mom must have been busily wrapping all night.

We followed Mom into the kitchen where she quickly threw her winter coat over her nursing scrubs and pulled out a pair of gloves. She slipped them on as well.

"I love you both," she said as she bent down to give each of us a hug and a kiss on the forehead. "I'm going to do everything I can to get out as early as possible. I left the emergency contact numbers on a sticky note on the fridge."

"We'll keep the house in one piece for you just this once," Colby replied sarcastically, causing Mom to crack a smile.

"Well, I appreciate that, Colby. If you and your sister could do your father and I a favor and keep up with shoveling the driveway today so we can pull in later, that would be fantastic." She replied as she headed into the garage.

"Oh, shoveling snow on Christmas Eve. Sounds like a lovely time," he replied snidely.

"You'll be fine," Mom yelled as she began to hop into her SUV. "It builds character." She gave a sarcastic wink and chuckled as she closed her car door. She pulled out into the snowy abyss, shutting the garage door with her remote in her car.

"Well, this sucks," Colby admitted as he turned to me and headed back into the kitchen.

"Agreed," was all I could muster as we both made our way to the cereal cabinet and poured ourselves bowls.

I glanced out the window from our kitchen overlooking the backyard which was a heavily wooded area. It was a dark grey overcast day and white-out snow conditions were ripping across the yard. I couldn't even see the tree line a mere 100 yards from the back of the house.

"Man, it's really coming down out there," I commented in a daze.

"Yeah, tell me about it. We're gonna spend all day shoveling snow out of the driveway," Colby answered in a mournful tone.

I wasn't looking forward to it any more than he was. We finished breakfast and glanced outside at the driveway through our living room window. You couldn't even see the tire tracks from where Mom had just pulled out.

"Do you think Dad will make it home on time?" I asked.

"I dunno," he replied with a sigh. "I sure hope so."

The snow was absolutely flying. Giant flakes came down at a frantic pace as the wind howled across the yard. I would be willing to bet if Dad had known this storm was coming, he wouldn't have taken the route, even with the rate he was being offered. I was just hopeful he and Mom would both make it home safe so we could spend Christmas together. I glanced over at Colby, who now had his head pressed against the window, looking like someone down on their luck.

"We should probably start up the fireplace," I suggested.

He glanced over and nodded. "I guess so."

Dad had taught us a couple winters ago how to start up our fireplace in case we were ever home alone during a storm and lost power. He had worked with us several times and ensured we had a full understanding of safety precautions and how to successfully get it started and maintained.

There was one thing I didn't want to have happen, and that was to lose power and not have a heat source. Power can frequently go out during these snowstorms.

Colby and I worked together and got the fireplace fired up. Warm heat began emanating from it as it crackled away.

"Success! We made fire!" Colby shouted with his arms raised in triumph.

I let out a chuckle. Sometimes Colby was okay to hang out with. With the fireplace stoked, it began to feel like Christmas, even without our parents being home. I turned on our family Bluetooth speaker and had Christmas music blaring through the house as we turned on all the Christmas decorations.

I think this snowstorm on Christmas Eve actually brought Colby and me closer together. We were getting along great, dancing and singing along with the Christmas carols.

After all our fun and excitement, we decided we had better get a jump on shoveling out the driveway for the first time. We both went upstairs and changed into our snowsuits and met back in the kitchen. We both decided to scarf down a cookie before we made our way outside.

Just as we were about to head out, the emergency cell phone that Mom and Dad got us last year started ringing.

I quickly ran in and answered. It was Dad. He wanted to see how we were doing and heard there was a snowstorm hitting us right now.

"Did Mom get called into work?" he asked.

"Yeah, she left a couple hours ago," I replied.

He apologized that we were home alone on Christmas Eve but was hurrying to make his way back to us as quickly and safely as he could.

"Did you guys get the fireplace going?" Dad inquired.

"Yep! Colby and I got it started about an hour ago with no issues," I answered in my best attempt at sounding like an adult.

"Excellent," he said pridefully.

It was great hearing his voice and knowing he was on his way back to us. Hopefully, the weather didn't slow him down too much. I told him that we were going to keep at the driveway throughout the day to make sure they could pull right in when they got home. Dad closed the call out by saying thank you and asked that I put him on speakerphone before telling us both he loved us, and he would be home this evening.

I think hearing how proud Dad was of us both motivated us to go out and get the driveway cleared out. It felt good.

We made our way out into the frozen tundra. As soon as we opened the garage door, we could see at least six inches of fresh snow had fallen already. The wind immediately began tearing into the garage, causing an immediate stinging on my face from the cold as we grabbed our shovels.

Luckily, our driveway wasn't that long. With both of us working on it, we could probably clear the whole thing out in about 30 minutes.

We immediately got to work. The snow was wet and heavy and kept coming down. By the time we were almost finished with the driveway, it looked like the area we'd just finished shoveling had another inch of snow on it. I knew this was going to be an all-day affair at this point.

Colby and I decided to head back inside once we had finished our first pass and take a break for a while.

"No sense in killing ourselves," he said as we made our way back into the garage, stomping the snow off the bottom of our boots.

His cheeks and nose were a rosy, red color. It was the kind of blustery cold day where the wind just cut through no matter how many layers you wore.

"Agreed. But hey, it was kinda fun," I lied.

I could sense Colby giving me a side-eye glance as we walked in the house. He said nothing but smirked as we went back inside our warm home to thaw out.

"I'm gonna go play some video games," Colby announced once he had shed his snow suit in our mud room.

"Okay. I'll probably watch TV or read or something," I suggested, a little upset, that Colby didn't want to hang out when we were getting along so well for once.

Once we made it upstairs, we went our separate ways. He quickly meandered into his room. I could hear his gaming system fire up.

I walked into my room and grabbed my newest book, which happened to be a story about Christmas. I hopped onto my bed and glanced out my window. The snow wasn't letting up. The brooding grey clouds, still looming over like a cold blanket, were a stark reminder that both my parents weren't home.

Snow is beautiful, but also so treacherous. I peeled open my book and began reading. After a while, I realized that shoveling the snow had worn me out. I set the book down and drifted off to sleep.

26.

When I woke up, everything had fallen silent in the house. Not hearing Colby yelling at his video games, I assumed he'd decided to take a nap as well.

I vaguely remember there being yelling in my dream, but I couldn't remember for the life of me what had happened. I glanced over at my computer and saw that it was powered off.

Huh, that's strange.

I rolled over and grabbed my TV remote. I tried to power it on, but nothing happened. I reached into my nightstand and grabbed my flashlight, just in case.

We must have lost power. Great.

I quickly rolled out of bed and made my way downstairs. The only light source in the house was supplied by our fireplace.

I wasn't sure how long I had been asleep, but the clouds had become even darker. I wasn't even sure how that was possible.

While it wasn't *pitch black*, it was still dark enough to make it difficult to see, and an ominous silence and stillness had fallen over the house.

I made my way over to the front window in the living room and looked at the driveway. It looked like we had never even shoveled it at this point.

Great…more back-breaking shoveling to do.

While looking out the window, I happened to notice that the driveway light at the McNeil house was on.

How can they have power, but not us? That's strange.

I figured I might as well go downstairs and check our breaker box. Once again, Dad's training came in handy. He'd always said he wanted us to be prepared for situations that we could control. He showed us how to operate the breaker box and make sure the switches were turned on, or to toggle them on and off to ensure we didn't have power.

I hurried through the hallway that led to our kitchen. It was almost pitch black in the hall. Normally, I would have needed my flashlight, but I had walked it so many times it was like muscle memory. I turned the corner toward our garage and hooked right. I opened the door that led to our basement.

It was pitch black. I could feel my heart racing. Even though this was a standard thing for me to do at this point, I still didn't like going into the dark basement alone. I turned my flashlight on and slowly made my way down the steps. Of course, I'd forgotten to put new batteries in my flashlight. It struggled to stay on, flickering on and off, and then dimming and brightening on its own.

I flipped the light switch at the top of the stairs on. It controlled all the lights in the basement. Of course, nothing happened. I was just hopeful that I wouldn't have to go down into the dark, scary basement alone. I let out a sigh of anguish as I plunged into the darkness.

As I made it to the bottom of the stairs, I fanned the flashlight around to make sure I was in the basement alone. I shouldn't be afraid of monsters in the basement at my age, but I still wanted to double-check. The coast was clear.

I scampered over to where the breaker box was located on the opposite wall, being careful not to run into anything as I made my way over. I opened the latch and pulled the door open. To my amazement, all the switches in the house had been turned off.

27.

This *had* to be Colby pulling a prank. He must have noticed me taking a nap and seized the opportunity to pull a fast one on me.

"Real funny, Colby!" I shouted as I reached forward and began flipping all the switches back on.

One by one, I could hear things turning back on as power surged through the house. The furnace immediately kicked back on as well. Finally, I flipped the switch for the basement. The lights immediately turned on, illuminating the entire room.

I let out an exasperated breath of relief. I felt proud of myself. And then...my heart sank.

"Hello, Kelsey," I heard a familiar sinister gravelly voice call out from behind me.

I felt a jolt of electric shock shoot up my spine and felt my breath instantly taken away. I didn't want to turn and look, but I knew I must.

Slowly, I turned toward the voice. There, standing on our family's card table stood Alfie. He had a sinister scowl plastered over his face, and a pair of scissors in hand. I felt sick. My heart was pounding, and I didn't want to believe this was possible.

"H-How? How did you get out?" I asked timidly.

"Never you mind that. I am going to make you wish you'd never brought us here," he answered as he quickly leapt from the table and onto the carpeted floor. He immediately began sprinting toward me with the scissors in hand.

I hesitated for a second before screaming as loud as my body could choke out before turning and running away. Alfie narrowly missed my leg with the scissors. I immediately rushed toward the staircase.

As I bounded up the stairs, I turned to look behind me and noticed Alfie was much faster than I would have thought. He wasn't far behind me at all.

"Come on, Kelsey! I just want to play!" he yelled with a maniacal laugh.

"Get away from me!" I shrieked, finally making it to the top of the stairs.

I went to slam the door shut, and as I did, Alfie came diving through the doorway just in time, sliding across the hardwood floor.

In the midst of his dive, he dropped the scissors. As he stumbled to get to his feet, I swiftly swung my foot at him, connecting and sending him flying across the mud room and slamming into the wall. He fell onto the shoe rack with a soft *thud* and lay motionless for a second.

I had slowly inched my way over to see if he was down for good when he groggily pushed himself back up, looking at me with the most frightening glare I had ever seen in my life.

"That...wasn't very nice," he said in a chilling tone as he brushed himself off.

Without hesitation, I turned and ran into the kitchen and began calling for Colby.

"Colby! Help! Where are you!" I yelled.

As I entered the hall leading to the living room, I noticed the closet had been opened. The shoebox that previously held the Jolly Elves lay on the floor with a hole punched out on the side. I hadn't noticed that in the darkness earlier.

I heard a bellow of eerie laughter coming from Alfie. I turned and saw him running after me, now midway through the kitchen. He hadn't bothered to pick up the scissors but was still barreling straight for me.

"Where are you going, Kelsey?" Alfie asked, cackling away as he began to gain ground on me.

Not able to stay still any longer, I ran down the hallway and toward the living room once again. I wasn't sure where the other two elves were, but I couldn't sit around and wait for them to show themselves. I needed to find Colby and find him quickly.

"Colby! Help me!" I shouted.

Yet again, there was no response from Colby.

28.

I continued to yell for Colby, getting more and more worried the longer I went without a response. I needed to go up to his room and see if he was there!

As I came sprinting through the living room, I heard a shrill, screeching yell come from beside me as I neared the Christmas tree. I stopped to look and saw Charlie the green elf jumping off the top of the tree. He came crashing down into the side of my head, clutching at my hair.

The force he hit me with was shocking, and I went tumbling sideways into our sofa. I began to wildly convulse, throwing my hands around everywhere and shaking my head to try to get him off me.

"Now I gotcha!" he shouted, tugging at my hair and causing a sharp searing pain to my scalp.

"No!" I yelled. "Get off me!" I quickly reached my hand back, grabbed hold of Charlie and desperately threw him off, sending him crashing back into the branches of the Christmas tree.

I climbed back to my feet, thinking I was in the clear. That thought quickly exited my mind when I felt myself yanked back down to the couch by my flowing golden locks.

I quickly turned my head back to see Alfie had caught up. His face sent a chill colder than the arctic air outside deep into the depths of my soul. He no longer looked angry. He was smiling.

I couldn't contain my fear any longer. I let out a blood-curdling scream as I fought to get Alfie off me. As I planted my right foot off the couch and struggled to wrangle the slippery elf out of my hair, I felt something grab ahold of my ankle.

I half-glanced down and saw that Charlie had already made his way back over. I was desperately fighting to get Alfie off me when Charlie gave a sharp yank on my ankle, sending me face-first back onto the couch.

I felt Charlie hastily begin climbing up my leg, trying to help his counterpart, Alfie. The strength they displayed was astonishing. *I had to get them off me. I had to make sure Colby was okay.*

I fought with everything I had in me. I pushed myself off the couch and Alfie yanked me back down by my hair once again. Charlie sprang forward like a monkey and forced my face back down into the couch cushions.

I suddenly heard a malevolent chuckle coming from the direction of the Christmas tree.

I turned to the side and saw Ernie, the white elf slowly walking over from the Christmas tree. In his hands, he held a candy cane that had been sharpened to a point. The disturbing expression of utter joy plastered over his face left me feeling scared out of my wits.

I continued to struggle and scream but wasn't making any progress. My heart raced. The three elves howled and giggled in a threatening and menacing manner. I *needed* to do something.

"Why are you doing this?" I cried.

"Why?" I heard Alfie call from above my head, pressing down and keeping a taut grip on my hair. "Because we can, that's why!"

"Yeah, all you ungrateful, snot-nosed kids taking us for granted over the years," Charlie said as he leaned closer to my face, keeping the pressure holding my head down.

"Toys. Toys. Toys," Ernie called out as he slowly closed in on the couch. "More toys. Make this. Make that. We elves are through with that."

"But you're just dolls!" I cried out.

"Oh-ho ho! Is that what you were told?" Ernie scoffed, his smile changing to an angry scowl once more. "No, that's just how we're dealt with when the North Pole is done with us. They turn us into toys!"

"Madame Trudeau saves our kind. She gives us life again!" Alfie sneered.

I couldn't believe what I was hearing. *This* was why Madame Trudeau did whatever magical spell to them the night we got them.

"The perfect front," Charlie beamed with a sinister grin. "B-but why?" I questioned nervously.

The three elves shot me a soul-piercing gaze, crude scowls forming over their little faces.

Charlie stepped forward with his arms crossed and a mean mug plastered over his face, "Madame Trudeau once loved Christmas...but over the years, she watched it go from a holiday meant to bring people together, to a commercialized greed pit."

A sullen silence befell the room as dread filled the air.

"And when she received word about what the fat man up north was doing to all of the Christmas creatures when he no longer had any use for them, she decided to take matters into her own hands," he continued. The other elves walked forward with their arms crossed.

"So, she struck a deal with the big guy to sell us as dolls, only she never told him about her true intentions with us," Alfie said coldly. He paused. "And that was to allow us to exact our revenge on ungrateful children like yourselves."

"Spoiled brats," added Charlie as the three elves chuckled eerily.

"And now you're going to pay!" Ernie wailed as he ran full sprint toward me, the sharpened candy cane pointed directly at me.

Alfie and Charlie began chanting "Pay!" over and over as Ernie closed in. This was my last chance to get away. I needed to pull a desperate move.

I pushed myself forward, pushing my feet off the armrest like a springboard, sending myself and the two elves on top of me toppling forward as I somersaulted off the couch, narrowly avoiding the rushing Ernie and the candy cane.

As I came down squarely on the floor, I felt the wind knocked out of me, but I didn't have time to spare. I fought my way to my feet, just as Ernie turned his attention to my new location.

"No!" I heard Alfie scream as I managed to shake both him and Charlie off, sending them catapulting across the room.

"You'll pay for that!" Ernie cried as he ran toward me like a knight entering a jousting competition.

If there was one advantage that I did have over them, it was my size.

Without thinking about it, my reflexes kicked in. I took a step and leapt over the top of the storming Ernie. I heard him go crashing into one of the wrapped Christmas gifts below the Christmas tree.

Now was my chance to get away and hopefully find Colby. I ran with every ounce of energy and strength that my legs would allow. I ran up the staircase, bounding up two steps at a time.

"Colby!" I yelled hoarsely, completely out of breath. My heart hadn't stopped racing in quite some time.

I could hear the elves down in the living room angrily giving chase again.

"Get her!" Charlie yelled from the bottom of the steps.

I didn't bother to turn and look. I didn't want to give them another second of time to catch up.

I quickly made my way to Colby's room. His door was wide open...

29.

As I turned the corner to enter Colby's room, I stopped dead in my tracks. There, in the center of the room, was a giant box. It had been sloppily wrapped in green wrapping paper with Santa faces all over it, and a red bow wound around the box.

"Colby?" I asked in bewilderment.

I was startled when I heard a groan come from inside the box. I was about to approach it, but was immediately snapped out of my state of confusion when I heard the chattering elves coming down the hall. I immediately turned back to the bedroom door, slamming it shut and locking it.

Moments later, I heard the elves angrily banging on the door with their tiny fists, screaming and hollering to let them in or they would find a way to break in.

"Just go away!" I shouted, my eyes welling up with tears.

The elves continued their tirade while I turned to the box in the center of Colby's room.

"Enjoy the present!" yelled one of the elves. They all erupted into laughter.

With my mind going a mile a minute, and my heart feeling like I had just run a marathon, I breathlessly began untying the bow around the box.

Once it was unraveled, I tossed it to the floor and immediately began tearing into the wrapping paper, tearing it off in huge chunks. On the side of the cardboard box, *Merry Christmas,* was written like chicken scratch in big font.

I quickly leaned over the top of the box and peeled back the packing tape before ripping the two box flaps open. There inside the box lay Colby. He had been tied up with strands of Christmas lights, and a piece of clear packing tape pressed over his mouth.

"Colby!" I shouted. He turned his head up to look at me and began grunting feverishly.

I quickly leaned into the box and ripped the tape off his mouth. He winced in pain.

"Kelsey! The elves! They...They're..." he said before I cut him off.

"Alive? Yeah, tell me something I don't know!" I said as I busily tried to yank his ankles free from the tightly-wrapped Christmas lights.

"I am sorry I didn't believe you! Please...Get me outta here!" Colby yelled as he began to squirm around inside the box.

"I'm trying!" I cried. It was too difficult, trying to lean over the box in his dark room to help him out.

I turned and ran over to the light switch in his room.

"Hey! Where are you going?" he cried.

I flipped the light on, and that seemed to calm him down a bit. I quickly used every ounce of strength I had to tip the box over so Colby could roll out and be in the open where I could get him freed easier.

"You kids better open up or we'll huff...and we'll puff..." I heard an elf say.

"That's not our line! We don't say that!" wailed another of the elves.

They immediately started bickering as I worked on the knotted-up cables around Colby's torso.

"I guess we're opting for the hard way," I heard one of the elves say as I finally made progress on the mess of wires constricting my brother.

"You won't like the hard way," I heard another reply.

I continued to ignore their taunts, and then things fell silent out in the hall. There was no more banging on the door, and no more yelling.

"Hurry up!" Colby pleaded, shaking back and forth on the floor.

"I almost have it. Just sit still!" I ordered.

Moments later, I managed to undo the knot that held it all together and immediately began to uncoil the Christmas lights that had pinned Colby's arms to his sides.

"How did this happen, Colby?" I asked.

"I don't know. They came in and jumped me while I was playing video games. I was caught off guard and before I knew what hit me, I was tangled up in this mess! How did you not hear the commotion?"

I hesitated at the thought for a moment, embarrassed. "I...uh.... I fell asleep."

"You were *sleeping?*" Colby whined as he shooed my hands away from his ankles and began unknotting them himself.

"I'm sorry! Okay?" I replied earnestly.

Finally, Colby managed to pull his ankles free and he leapt up to his feet.

"Those stupid elves. What are we going to do now?" he asked, his voice shaken from everything that had just happened.

"I...I don't know," I answered honestly.

That was the truth. I didn't know what to do. None of this should be possible. But here we were, in the midst of a blizzard and locked in the house with sadistic elves looking to ruin Christmas, or worse...ruin us.

"At least the door is locked for now," I said, trying to present a false confidence for Colby.

"Oh, great. We're trapped like rats!" he complained.

"Listen, they can't get in here. We should just wait this out until Mom or Dad gets home," I said trying to not only reassure Colby, but myself as well.

Colby agreed, and we both wound up taking a seat on his bed. This day had gone from bad to worse. Starting with the storm, and now the day furthering into disarray with the sadistic Jolly Elves coming back to life, some sort of sick vengeance on their mind.

Colby and I tried to crack a couple of lighthearted jokes to make ourselves feel better, but none of them really seemed to be hitting the way we would like. Deep down we were both struggling to wrap our brains around how any of this was possible.

I glanced out Colby's bedroom window. The snow was still dumping outside as the unforgiving, dark grey clouds loomed overhead.

"Christmas, eh?" Colby joked.

I cracked a warm, yet broken smile. "Christmas."

As the tension continued to fill the room, Colby and I both reacted to hearing noises coming from what sounded like underneath the floor of his room.

"Uh...what was that?" he asked, his voice dripping with apprehension.

I was just as startled as he was. "I-I don't know."

Things fell silent once again, leaving us both literally on the edge of our seats. That seat being Colby's bed.

The noises began once again. It sounded like metal scraping on metal coming from underneath Colby's bedroom floor.

"Kelsey! What's going on?" he whispered anxiously.

"Will you shut up?" I demanded, trying to get a better listen.

Before either of us fully realized what was happening, the register for Colby's heating vent popped out of its place next to his bed and came crashing back down onto the hardwood floor with a *clank*. We yelped in fright.

Both of us inhaled deep breaths of shock from the noise and what we were now looking at.

Crawling out of the air vent were the three Jolly Elves, their faces once again contorted by rage-filled glares as they dragged themselves into Colby's room.

30.

Neither Colby nor I could believe what we were seeing. I don't think either of us ever would have thought that the elves would be smart enough to figure out how to navigate the air vents like this. They were calculated and crafty, and that was just as scary as their demeanor.

The three elves slowly approached us. Alfie had once again acquired the pair of scissors from earlier. Ernie was wielding his sharpened candy cane, and Charlie trotted forward carrying a splintered-off branch from the Christmas tree.

"We've got you now!" Alfie warned.

"You can't escape us," Charlie added as they slowly moved forward.

"What are we gonna do?" Colby asked tugging nervously at my arm.

"Run!" I yelled, turning toward his bedroom door.

"Get 'em!" I heard Ernie yell behind us.

I reached the door and twisted and turned at the knob, forgetting I had locked it earlier, wasting precious seconds.

I hurriedly unlocked the door and let Colby pass through first. I slid out the door and slammed it shut just as the trio of elves had reached it. I heard the scissors collide with the door, before hearing Alfie tug them back out of it.

We couldn't lock them in the room from outside, but we had slowed them down. I turned to run down the hall. Colby was already making a beeline down the stairs.

I quickly met him down at the bottom of the steps in the living room.

"What are we going to do now?" Colby asked.

I had to take a moment to think. All the chaos had really jumbled my brain. Colby was clearly looking to me to be a big sister and take the lead. I had to come up with a plan, and I needed to think fast.

I glanced over at the antique clock resting on our mantle above the fireplace. It was only 3:16 PM. We couldn't wait for Mom or Dad to get home. We had to fight.

Wait...the fireplace!

I had a light bulb moment but didn't want to speak too loudly in case the elves heard my plan. I pointed to the fireplace. Colby shot me a confused look.

"We need to get them in the fireplace," I whispered.

"And how are we going to do that exactly?" he breathed back.

I looked around the room. I knew we didn't have much time before the elves had either managed to open our door or decided to go through the vents once again. I racked my brain, but nothing came forth.

I looked at an ornament on our Christmas tree. It was an ornament with Marv and Harry from *Home Alone* after they had gone through a torturous night trying to rob Kevin McCallister's house. *That was it!*

"We need to set a trap," I said quietly.

"We don't have time!" Colby whispered back urgently, becoming a little bit hoarse.

"Then we need to move fast," I called out as I ran for the kitchen.

I had an idea. It was time to get rid of these elves once and for all.

I went to the cabinet next to our fridge and pulled out the cling wrap Mom used when putting away leftovers.

"This should work," I whispered excitedly, feeling extremely confident we were going to nab these mischievous elves.

"What is that going to do?" Colby questioned, nervously eyeing the cling wrap in my hands.

"You'll see!" I declared. "I've seen this in prank videos online before."

Colby looked irritated. "Oh great! Putting our lives in the hands of prank videos now."

"Just shut up and help me!" I said as I rushed back toward the living room.

This plan just might work! It wasn't quite as crafty as *Home Alone* but would hopefully, do the trick!

"What good is this going to do if the elves use the vents again?" Colby stammered.

"Let's just hope they are in such a frenzy, that they don't think about it!" I replied nervously.

I was hoping and praying this would work. These elves were very smart, but hopefully, they'd be cocky right now, thinking they had us on the run.

As we made our way to the staircase, I heard a chair being dragged across the hardwood floor in Colby's room. We didn't have much time.

I instructed Colby to pull the cling wrap tight across the bottom of the staircase.

"Do you really think this is going to work?" he asked as he helped stretch the sticky plastic across the bottom of the stairs.

"I sure hope so," I replied.

Once we had it stretched far enough out, I cut the cling wrap free from the box, and we smoothed it out across the wall. In the low light, it was absolutely invisible.

This is perfect.

Moments after we had the trap set, I heard my bedroom door opening.

Shortly after, I heard one of the elves say, "Oh children," in a slow drawn-out, eerie voice.

My overconfidence was showing, and I couldn't help but quote *Home Alone* when I said: "We're really scared," and "You better come get us."

Evil laughter echoed through the hallway. I pulled Colby away from the staircase by his arm and stopped in the center of the living room.

We watched in horror as the devilish Jolly Elves climbed down the steps, their creepy stares honed in on us. Even though the trap was set, it was still frightening to see these little creatures moving around on their own.

"Never to worry, children. It'll all be over soon!" I heard Charlie say.

"Hey! What the—?" I heard Ernie call out as the three elves walked right into the cling wrap, punching into it and falling helplessly to the floor.

"Yes!" I yelled in triumph.

I knew the job wasn't over yet. I quickly rushed over to the staircase landing and tried to roll them up in the cling wrap.

As soon as I made it there, Alfie managed to tear himself free of the cling wrap, yanking his scissors away as well. He darted across the room.

"No! Colby! Get him!" I yelled as I rolled the other two angry, yelling elves into a burrito of cling wrap.

I turned to look back and saw Colby narrowly miss nabbing Alfie as he darted under the Christmas tree and hid behind all the Christmas gifts.

"Great! Now what?" he asked impatiently.

I didn't have an answer. If Alfie hadn't had the scissors, we could just pull him out and it would be done, but I didn't want to risk us getting hurt. I ignored the angry yells from Charlie and Ernie, doing my best to come up with a plan.

I heard some rustling come from inside the Christmas tree's branches. We needed to come up with a plan fast before Alfie did.

I ordered Colby to stand guard and be careful. I had an idea. Colby didn't seem to like waiting, but I told him we couldn't give Alfie an opportunity to free the other two elves.

He agreed, and I quickly sprinted to the kitchen once more. I scurried over to the drawer next to our stove and pulled out a couple of oven mitts that our parents used when handling hot pans.

I slid them over my arms, doing a lobster pinch with them to test their functionality.

"Better than nothing," I whispered as I made my way back to the living room.

All my hopes were dashed when I saw Alfie on Colby's shoulder with the scissors placed against the front of his neck ready to strike.

"Stop right there!" Alfie ordered.

I did as he said. "Please don't hurt him!" I wailed.

"Do as I say, and he will be fine," Alfie hissed. "Free my brothers, and I will free your brother."

"Don't do it, Kels!" Colbie warned.

"Shut up, you!" Alfie sneered as he crouched, ready to attack Colby at any moment. "Let my brothers go…now!"

I couldn't let Alfie hurt Colby. I told him I would free the other elves, and just not to hurt him. An evil smile formed over Alfie's face. I took the oven mitts off and tossed them onto the couch.

I had a sick feeling in the pit of my stomach that if I complied with Alfie, both me and Colby were going to be in some serious trouble. I had to think on my feet and come up with yet another plan.

I walked over toward the rolled-up elves, who were now laughing hysterically. I scooped them up and walked back toward my brother and Alfie.

"Yes…that's it!" Alfie jeered.

I had an idea. It was an all-or-nothing move I needed to take. If the plan didn't work this time, Colby was in danger. But I knew I had to do something.

I slowly approached to the two of them and lurched forward as if I were getting ready to set the two elves down. Suddenly I shot up and, like a javelin, threw the bundled-up elves as hard as I could toward Colby's shoulder.

The move caught Alfie off guard as they collided with him, sending him flying backward off Colby's shoulder. The scissors fell to the floor.

"Colby! Quick! Get him!" I yelled.

This time, Colby didn't miss the opportunity. He aggressively lunged face-first toward the floor, falling on top of the stunned Alfie.

"Ow!" I heard Colby yell. "He bit me!"

"You are darn right! Get your filthy hands off me!" Alfie barked angrily.

I hurried over to help my struggling brother. With my help, Colby was finally able to change his grip and wrap his hand around Alfie's torso.

Alfie continued to yell and scream threats at both of us as I scooped up his two brothers in my hand.

"It's now or never," I told Colby as we hurried to the fireplace which was still crackling away.

I pulled the protective fence away from the front of it, and we tossed the elves into the inferno. Immediately, ear-piercing squeals bellowed from the elves as I placed the protective gate shut in front of it once more.

The flames erupted into a sea of red, green, and white hues before a loud pop that sounded like a gunshot erupted from the fireplace. Colby and I both shielded ourselves with our arms, bracing for impact after the noise, but then things fell silent.

We both uncovered our faces. The fire was back to burning like normal and the elves were now just a distant, horrible memory. The aroma of peppermint emanated from the fireplace, filling our living room with the sweet scent.

"We did it!" I yelled excitedly, giving Colby the biggest and tightest hug I had ever given him.

"Thank God!" Colby exclaimed, returning the bear hug.

When we broke our embrace, I took a moment to take it all in. The energy in the house had shifted. It felt like home again. The weight of the world was finally lifted from my shoulders, and I felt like I could breathe freely once more.

The saying was always to have a very merry Christmas. This year, I guess you could say this was a very scary Christmas.

"Kelsey, look!" Colby exclaimed, pointing out the front window.

To my shock, the winter storm had finally subsided. The grey foreboding clouds still hung overhead, but no more snow fell.

I felt a wave of excitement rush over me. I could tell Colby was in the same boat. We decided our work wasn't done and wanted to be responsible. We cleaned up the mess from today's battle, putting everything back in its rightful place.

"Let's not mention any of this to Mom or Dad," I told Colby.

"Agreed," he said timidly.

I took the old shoebox the elves had escaped from and threw that into the fireplace to fully erase any trace of them from this house. Then, Colby and I went outside and cleared the driveway of any snow that had been covering it, eagerly anticipating our parents' arrival.

31.

We had finally finished all the household chores and cleanup and decided to kick back and watch *Home Alone 2* on TV while we waited. We made it a short way into the movie when a set of headlights illuminated the darkness outside.

Colby and I both raced to the front window. It was Mom!

We ran to the front door, and met her with giant hugs, seemingly catching her off guard as she let out a laugh of surprise and returned the hug.

"Thank you for taking care of the house," she said happily. "I'm glad to see you both didn't run into any trouble."

Colby and I shared cautious glances before looking at Mom with bright smiles.

"Nope, it was a pretty boring day," Colby finally said, garnering laughter from all of us.

We all reconvened in the living room shortly after Mom had gone upstairs and changed out of her work clothes. As soon as she sat on the couch, another set of headlights came pulling into the driveway.

"Perfect timing," she said with a laugh, grunting with effort as she tried to get up off the sofa.

We all made our way into the kitchen and gave Dad a big hug as he excitedly burst through the door and into the house.

Our family was finally together for Christmas. We wound up finishing the night by watching Christmas movies and taking in the moment by staring at our Christmas tree. I stared at the fireplace and knew I would forever have the memory from earlier today etched into my brain.

It wound up being an early night for all of us. I think we were all exhausted. My parents had been working all day, and Colby and I had won our battle with the elves on top of shoveling the driveway twice.

I flopped into bed and immediately fell asleep.

It felt like I had just shut my eyes when Colby came barging into my room.

"Kelsey! Kelsey!" he said enthusiastically. "Get up! It's Christmas morning!"

I sluggishly wiped my eyes with a yawn and looked out my window. Sure enough, the sun was already up and beating down over our snow-covered yard.

Colby darted out of my room and quickly headed downstairs.

While I share the same enthusiasm as Colby, I just wanted to sleep a little longer.

Things could be worse though.

I rolled out of bed and met my family down in the basement. There was something so magical about the initial moment you meet your family around the Christmas tree first thing in the morning on Christmas Day.

The stockings were stuffed, the tree was lit up, and my parents had turned on Christmas music. Both of them were sitting on the sofa in their bathrobes and house slippers, sipping from their coffee mugs.

"Merry Christmas, Kelsey," both said with jovial smiles.

"Merry Christmas," I replied eagerly, with the biggest smile I'd had in a week.

"Well...what are you kids waiting for? Dig in!" Dad declared with a chuckle.

Colby wasted no time dumping out his stocking and seeing all the neat little toys and candy bars as they toppled out all over the floor.

I followed his lead and did the same before Mom got off the couch and handed me my first gift.

"Here, Kelsey," she said, holding the gift out to me with a warm smile. "Open this one first."

I took hold of the box that had been wrapped in blue wrapping paper with white snowflakes all over it. I instinctively tore the paper away. It appeared to be just a plain, brown cardboard box.

"Open it!" Mom said, elation filling her voice. She had a gleeful smile as she sat back on the couch next to Dad.

I peeled the tape from the top of the box and parted the two flaps. Inside the box was the trio of Nutcracker dolls I had wanted last week. I felt a surge of excitement. I looked up at my mom and eagerly said thank you.

I then looked back down at the Nutcracker dolls in the box, admiring them.

Suddenly a jolt of fear surged through my entire body. I let out a frightened shriek as I dropped the box to the floor.

The middle Nutcracker doll had winked at me.

A NOTE FROM THE AUTHOR

I just want to say thank you to all who have continued to stick with me and have helped grow the Scareville Army into what it is slowly becoming. It means the world to me that you all continue to support me and allow me to have my imagination run wild and bring fun, yet spooky stories for you all to enjoy! Christmas has always been a major holiday in my life, as well as with my family. I wanted to bring the fun of Christmas with a splash of terrifying horror, and hope that you all have enjoyed *A Very Scary Christmas*. Each and every one of you reading this means the world to me. I just want everyone to truly understand how much this all really means. I am so excited for the future of Scareville and look forward to bringing even more spooky stories your way!

Be sure to follow Scareville Books on Facebook, Instagram, and TikTok!

Stay up to date with the Scareville series!
#1. Welcome to Scareville
#2. How to Create a Monster
#3 Monsters of Mt. Hope
#4 A Very Scary Christmas

And be on the lookout for the fifth book from the Scareville
Series:
#5 Got Ghosts?

I WANT
YOU
FOR
SCAREVILLE
EST
20
25
ARMY
JOIN NOW!

THE END?

Not if you want to dive into more of Crystal Lake Publishing's Tales from the Darkest Depths!

For our mature horror books, check out our amazing website and online store or download our latest catalog here. https://geni.us/CLPCatalog

We always have great new projects and content on the website to dive into, as well as a newsletter, behind the scenes options, social media platforms, our own dark fiction shared-world series and our very own webstore. Our webstore even has categories specifically for KU books, non-fiction, anthologies, and of course more novels and novellas.

Readers...

Thank you for reading *A Very Scary Christmas*. We hope you enjoyed this entry into the Scareville Universe.

If you have a moment, please review *A Very Scary Christmas* at the store where you bought it.

Help other readers by telling them why you enjoyed this book. No need to write an in-depth discussion. Even a single sentence will be greatly appreciated. Reviews go a long way to helping a book sell, and is great for an author's career. It'll also help us to continue publishing quality books.

Thank you again for taking the time to journey with Crystal Lake Publishing.
You will find links to all our social media platforms on our Linktree page.
https://linktr.ee/CrystalLakePublishing

Follow us on Amazon:

MISSION STATEMENT

Since its founding in August 2012, Crystal Lake has quickly become one of the world's leading publishers of Dark Fiction and Horror books. In 2023, Crystal Lake officially transitioned into an entertainment company, joining several other divisions, genres, and imprints, including Torrid Waters, Crystal Lake Comics, Crystal Lake Games, Crystal Lake Kids, and many more.

While we strive to present only the highest quality fiction and entertainment, we also endeavour to support authors along their writing journey. We offer our time and experience in non-fiction projects, as well as author mentoring and services, at competitive prices.

With several Bram Stoker Award wins and many other wins and nominations (including the HWA's Specialty Press Award), Crystal Lake Publishing puts integrity, honor, and respect at the forefront of our publishing operations.

We strive for each book and outreach program we spearhead to not only entertain and touch or comment on issues that affect our readers, but also to strengthen and support the Dark Fiction field and its authors.

Not only do we find and publish authors we believe are destined for greatness, but we strive to work with men and women who endeavour to be decent human beings who care more for others than themselves, while still being hard working, driven, and passionate artists and storytellers.

Crystal Lake Publishing is and will always be a beacon of what passion and dedication, combined with overwhelming teamwork and respect, can accomplish. We endeavour to know each and every one of our readers, while building personal relationships with our authors, reviewers, bloggers, podcasters, bookstores, and libraries.

We will be as trustworthy, forthright, and transparent as any business can be, while also keeping most of the headaches away from our authors, since it's our job to solve the problems so they can stay in a creative mind. Which of course also means paying our authors.

We do not just publish books, we present to you worlds within your world, doors within your mind, from talented authors who sacrifice so much for a moment of your time.

There are some amazing small presses out there, and through collaboration and open forums we will continue to support other presses in the goal of helping authors and showing the world what quality small presses are capable of accomplishing. No one wins when a small press goes down, so we will always be there to support hardworking, legitimate presses and their authors. We don't see Crystal Lake as the best press out there, but we will always strive to be the best, strive to be the most interactive and grateful, and even blessed press around. No matter what happens over time, we will also take our mission very seriously while appreciating where we are and enjoying the journey.

What do we offer our authors that they can't do for themselves through self-publishing?

We are big supporters of self-publishing (especially hybrid publishing), if done with care, patience, and planning. However, not every author has the time or inclination to do market research, advertise, and set up book launch strategies. Although a lot of authors are successful in doing it all, strong small presses will always be there for the authors who just want to do what they do best: write.

What we offer is experience, industry knowledge, contacts and trust built up over years. And due to our strong brand and trusting fanbase, every Crystal Lake Publishing book comes with weight of respect. In time our fans begin to trust our judgment and will try a new author purely based on our support of said author.

With each launch we strive to fine-tune our approach, learn from our mistakes, and increase our reach. We continue to assure our authors that we're here for them and that we'll carry the weight of the launch and dealing with third parties while they focus on their strengths—be it writing, interviews, blogs, signings, etc.

We also offer several mentoring packages to authors that include knowledge and skills they can use in both traditional and self-publishing endeavours.

We look forward to launching many new careers.

This is what we believe in. What we stand for. This will be our legacy.

Welcome to Crystal Lake Publishing—Where Stories Come Alive!